THE LEGACY SERIES

SERIES TITLES

Release of Information
Kali White VanBaale

Neon Steel
Jennifer Maritza McCauley

How We Do Things Here
Matt Cashion

The Divide
Evan Morgan Williams

Yes, No, I Don't Know
Kathryn Gahl

The Price of Their Toys
John Loonam

The Caged Man
Calvin Mills

A Day Doesn't Go By When I Don't Have Regrets
J. Malcolm Garcia

These Are My People
Steve Fox

We Should Be Somewhere by Now
Stephen Tuttle

Burner and Other Stories
Katrina Denza

The Plan of Chicago
Barry Pearce

Trust Issues
K.P. Davis

Adult Children
Laurence Klavan

Guardians & Saints
Diane Josefowicz

Western Terminus: Stories and A Novella
Michael Keefe

In Kali White VanBaale's new collection, a national outage of Target checkout software brings about salvation and downfall in equal measure, the Iowa State Fair caricature tent sets the scene for a quiet yet monumental reconciliation, and a library book a decade overdue serves as a reminder of a dark secret. Compelling, devastating, yet often bleakly funny, *Release of Information* explores the depths that lie behind every "Midwest nice" smile.

—SEAN ADAMS
author of *The Thing in the Snow*

RELEASE of INFORMATION

and other linked stories

Kali White VanBaale

CORNERSTONE PRESS

UNIVERSITY OF WISCONSIN-STEVENS POINT

Cornerstone Press, Stevens Point, Wisconsin 54481
Copyright © 2026 Kali White VanBaale
www.uwsp.edu/cornerstone

Printed in the United States of America by
Point Print and Design Studio, Stevens Point, Wisconsin

Library of Congress Control Number: 2025950986
ISBN: 978-1-968148-24-9

This is a work of fiction. Names, characters, businesses, places, events, and incidents are either the products of the author's imagination or used in a fictitious manner. Any resemblance to actual persons, living or dead, or actual events is purely coincidental.

Cornerstone Press titles are produced in courses and internships offered by the Department of English at the University of Wisconsin–Stevens Point.

DIRECTOR & PUBLISHER
Dr. Ross K. Tangedal

EXECUTIVE EDITORS
Jeff Snowbarger, Freesia McKee

EDITORIAL DIRECTOR
Brett Hill

SENIOR EDITORS
Paige Biever, Ellie Atkinson

PRESS STAFF
Lillian Kulbeck, Ari Pinder, Samantha Bjork, Sophie McPherson, Madison Schultz, Autumn Vine, McKenna Bartel, John Evans, Gwen Goetter, Brian Grzesik, Sam Zajkowski

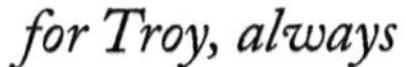

for Troy, always

Stories

Hyatt at the Arch

The hotel lights blinked once, then extinguished. The television screen, blaring the evening news, went dark with a single crackle of static. Jay Morton looked up from his file of open papers across his lap and waited. The girls simultaneously switched on their phone flashlights, and Tricia, napping on the bed next to Jay, lifted her head. "What happened?" she asked, her voice thick and drowsy.

One of the girls directed the beam of her phone light directly into Jay's eyes, blinding him. "Hey," he said, holding up a hand.

"Sorry."

Claudia. Jay recognized her higher, squeaky voice. She directed the beam to the other side of the room.

"Claudia! God!" Lydia this time, now holding her hand up to shield her eyes, just as Jay had.

They sat in silence a few moments longer, but the darkness persisted.

"Oh, come on," Tricia said, fully upright now. "Seriously?"

Jay closed the file and swung his legs over the side of the bed. He felt his way to the bathroom and tried each switch along the way, but nothing. Claudia followed with her phone light.

"Call the front desk," she said behind him.

Jay turned and bumped into her. "Yeah, I will."

She stepped out of his way and stumbled over a small suitcase splayed open on the floor—likely her own as the messier twin.

"So much for the five-star reviews," Tricia said, fanning herself with her hand as if the room were already growing hot, which it wasn't.

Jay turned on his own phone light and studied the landline phone on the desk. This was supposed to be a fun work-slash-family weekend getaway during the girls' spring break, a conference he attended every year. He'd suggested his wife and pre-pubescent daughters come along this time, but it had been a hard sell despite hyping tours of the Arch and Grant's Farm. He'd surely get shit for this inconvenience.

Jay squinted at the myriad of buttons until he finally located the "front desk" label in tiny print. He pushed the button and waited with the receiver pressed to his ear as it pulsed, now detecting a small rise in the stuffy room air himself. St. Louis in March was so much warmer than Minneapolis. When they'd left that morning, it had been drizzling and chilly. The temperature jumped almost twenty degrees as soon as they'd crossed the Missouri line.

Jay let the phone beep a few more times and hung up. "No one answered. I'll have to go down to the lobby."

Tricia sighed and laid back down. Jay knew she was exhausted from a long week at the clinic and driving the girls to activities. He felt guilty for pressuring her into the trip.

"Can I come?" Claudia asked.

"Just let Dad take care of it," Tricia said.

Jay opened the door and poked his head into the sixth-floor hallway, surprised to find it barely lit by weak emergency lights along the floor. A few other guests had wandered out of their rooms.

"Seems like the entire floor is out." Jay pulled his head back from the cracked door.

"How long will this take?" Lydia asked. "I need to charge my phone."

"Hopefully not very long," Jay said. "I'll be right back." He closed the door and fell into step with an older man walking toward the elevators.

"You, too?" The man said.

"Yep."

They were surprised to find the elevators still in working order and waited as the digital number screens painstakingly moved down, stopping on every floor for minutes at a time.

The man tucked his hands into his trouser pockets and rocked back on his heels. "Here on vacation?"

"Kind of a work-fun weekend," Jay answered, and pretended to send a text, though he was really just typing nonsense in a Note. He hated small talk, especially with strangers. A requirement in his profession, and one he'd come to loathe in every aspect of life. Tricia was the opposite. She had the type of personality to ask every cashier and Uber driver their life story, and then promptly tell them how to live it better. She would get into a car saying something like, "Take Fifth Street, please—it's faster than Grand," and get out saying things like, "Good luck with your studies! Tell that professor you just need an extension for two days, and make sure he understands how sick your baby has been." Jay could barely be bothered to mumble a hello and goodbye.

The man whistled for a few seconds, then paused. He was going to ask what Jay did, without a doubt, so Jay held his phone screen closer to his face and furrowed his brow, hoping to convey a hint to leave him alone.

"What kind of work are you in?"

Jay held back an annoyed sigh. "I'm an anesthesiologist. Here for a medical seminar."

"Ah!" The old man said. "I've had this weird bump on the top of my foot for a month now, and it just keeps getting bigger. What do you think it could be?"

Jay looked at him and blinked. "I have no idea. I'm an *anesthesiologist*." He drew the word out slowly even though he knew it made him sound like a dick. Tricia, a dermatologist, would've diagnosed him right in the elevator.

But the man didn't seem to notice. "I was in insurance, myself. Forty years, and just retired last year. Here with my wife for our fifty-second wedding anniversary. We're doing one of them paddle wheel river tours. I'm Howard."

They shook hands without Jay offering his name in the hopes of preventing further engagement.

"You married?" Howard asked.

Jesus, where was Tricia when he needed her? He nodded and replied, "Going on twenty."

The elevator doors mercifully opened and revealed a rowdy group of young men in tuxedos. Jay squeezed in next to Howard—no way was he waiting for another one—just before the doors closed. The hot air inside smelled of sweat and booze.

"You all in a wedding or something?" Howard asked the men and laughed.

Jay discreetly rolled his eyes at the inane joke. The men looked barely old enough to attend a prom, let alone stand up in a wedding.

"Yeah," one of the young men answered. "My brother got married today. Reception is downstairs."

The elevator finally reached the ground level, and the doors opened to the lobby, which teemed with more wedding guests spilling out of a nearby ballroom.

Jay and Howard separated in the crowd, and each found a spot in different lines at the front desk. Jay's phone dinged with a text. Tricia.

What did the front desk say?

Jay shuffled forward in the line as he typed a reply.

Busy down here. Waiting to talk to someone.

She replied with an eye roll emoji.

Jay mindlessly scrolled through his social media apps, impatiently shifting his weight from one foot to the other until it was his turn.

"Welcome to Hyatt at the Arch, how can I help you?" a tired-looking attendant greeted him.

Jay explained their loss of electricity, and she apologized for the inconvenience, then made a series of monotone phone calls bordering on irritated.

"Maintenance is on its way up," she finally said.

Jay thanked her and escaped the lobby without Howard spotting him.

He reentered the elevator with a couple this time, who thankfully huddled in the corner, whispering to each other and completely ignoring him. The elevator stopped on the third floor, and the doors opened. There, a group of women in identical pink dresses sat on a round, velvet-covered settee, talking loudly with a bride in the middle, who silently stared straight ahead. She and Jay made eye contact and held it for a few strange, uncomfortable seconds until the doors closed.

Back in the room, Jay found the girls sitting next to the window overlooking the Arch and the flat, brown Mississippi River. Tricia was now upright, tapping away on her laptop.

"Front desk is sending up a maintenance person," Jay said.

"When?" Tricia asked.

"I don't . . . I didn't think to ask."

Tricia huffed and returned to typing, her neck and cheeks flushing with annoyance, at the electrical inconvenience or his ineptitude, hard to tell.

Now the room was uncomfortably stuffy, and Jay pulled off his sneakers and socks. He tried to think of something to say to his family, to start a conversation, to use this time to talk, really *talk*, to each other, but the silence only fattened and crowded out ideas. Tricia sighed every thirty seconds or so, as if on a timer.

His seminar started tomorrow morning, and Tricia and the girls planned to visit the City Museum, saving the Arch for when he could join them in the afternoon. The following day was Grant's Farm, then The Dinner Detective theater. When he and Tricia—or rather, Tricia had—created the schedule a few weeks ago, he'd been agreeable and thought it sounded fun. But as it usually went in their family, it only took one hiccup to derail everyone's mood and suck any enjoyment from everything else thereafter.

Someone knocked sharply at the door. "Maintenance," a man's voice called.

Jay rose and opened the door. Tricia set aside her laptop and followed.

"Hi," a young man said. "We're not going to get power restored to this floor tonight. We're moving everyone to other rooms."

"Are you kidding me?" Tricia said, behind Jay now. He discreetly shifted to block her.

"Yeah," the maintenance man said, "we're really sorry. If you check back in with the front desk, they'll get you a new room and key."

Tricia pointed at him and bumped Jay's shoulder. "We'd better get a discount for this inconvenience."

Jay gave the guy an apologetic look and quickly closed the door. "Jesus, Trish, calm down," he said.

"Don't tell me to calm down," she snapped. "This is fucking ridiculous."

"Mom, quarter," Lydia said, holding out her hand while still staring at her phone.

Tricia grabbed her purse from the desk and removed her wallet. She slapped a one-dollar bill onto Lydia's palm. "Paying in advance. Because this is going to be a long fucking day."

The girls exchanged smirks. Tricia flopped back onto the bed and flung an arm over her eyes.

Jay slipped on a pair of sandals and left the room. The depths of his wife's irritations with life remained a vast, overwhelming abyss to him.

He once again waited several minutes for the elevator, though thankfully alone this time. Back in line at the front desk, wedding guests still drunkenly milled about, stepping on his bare toes. The same desk attendant switched them to a new room on the tenth floor, with another apology in the same tired voice, and gave him a new room key.

Jay returned to the elevators in what was starting to feel like a personal version of Groundhog Day.

Sometimes the mundane repetitions of life felt like they were grinding him down to a small, indistinct nub. The same routines, work conferences, and holiday traditions. The same inconveniences, struggles, complaints, and fights. Always waiting in line for something.

But occasionally, the smallest deviation felt noteworthy, even disturbingly disruptive. Like a few days ago, when he'd arrived at his office as usual and discovered he'd accidentally grabbed Tricia's laptop bag—a black leather messenger in a slightly different style than his own—from the bench by the back door. The realization had jolted him in a strange way he couldn't identify, so much so that he'd thought to himself, *Well, this has never happened before.*

In all their years together, he'd never once looked inside Tricia's bag, had never even considered it because it was *her* private work bag, just like his own. But in that small moment of deviation, he'd looked. He'd set it on his desk and opened it out of curiosity. In addition to her laptop, he found a yellow legal pad with notes on two new patients (one with psoriasis, one with eczema), a pen light identical to his own, a bottle of hand sanitizer, a tampon, and finally, perplexingly, a children's picture book. *Stellaluna*—about a little fruit bat—checked out from the Rochester Public Library.

When he opened the book, he found the check-out receipt in the front cover. It was thirteen years overdue. Not days. Not weeks. Not months. *Years*. He'd done the math. Eleven years equaled 4,745 days. At twenty-five cents a day, the grand total of the overdue fine would be $1,186.25.

His wife—who had created a detailed itinerary for their two-day trip to St. Louis and texted it to Jay and the girls, who alphabetized her spice rack, and had dental cleanings on their shared calendar a year in advance—kept an overdue children's book in her work bag for thirteen years from a public library in a city they hadn't lived in since the girls were babies.

Jay had no memory of ever seeing Tricia read that particular book to the girls, and why she'd kept it—carried it around with her daily—was confounding. It was so out of character for her that he might as well have discovered a packet of heroin tucked next to the tampon. If it had been someone like his troubled younger sister, Kara, he wouldn't have been the least bit surprised by a decade's overdue book, or heroin, or both, despite her recent efforts to get and stay clean.

But not Tricia. She was unfailingly responsible. Dependable. Predictable. All the years they'd been married, the library book was the most mysterious and irresponsible thing she'd ever done, and even though Jay was too cowardly to ask her about it, he couldn't stop thinking about it.

He got back on the elevator alone, bracing himself for Tricia's assured ire at the room switch situation. They'd have to re-pack all their belongings, lug them up to the tenth floor, and unpack a second time. Even *he* was annoyed now. The elevator glided past the first and second floors and stopped at three, opening to reveal the seating area that had previously been clogged with bridesmaids in pink dresses, like a patch of skin. Only the bride remained, still sitting on the round settee with her head bowed, shoulders shaking. She was crying.

Just as Jay started to slink into the corner, she looked up at him. They made eye contact, like they'd done before, and fresh tears streamed down her shiny cheeks. The doors began to close, and at the last second Jay stuck his hand out and pushed them back open. He stepped off the elevator and approached her.

"Are you okay?" The doors gently closed behind him, and the elevator moved on.

The bride dabbed the corners of her eyes with a tissue and laughed ruefully. "Sure." Her face crumpled and she turned her head to the side.

Jay stood dumbly, unsure what to do next. "Do you want me to wait here with you?"

She nodded.

Jay sat next to her on the soft velvet cushion. "Did something happen? Can I . . . call someone?"

She shook her head, rustling the layers of tulle in her waist-length veil. "I just need a minute."

Jay clasped his hands and waited.

"Weddings are stressful," he finally said, unable to come up with anything more profound or comforting without knowing the actual problem. "But you look very pretty. Your dress is beautiful."

"It's a designer gown," she said, sniffling. "It even has a name. It's called the 'Bijou.'"

"Oh. Interesting."

She smoothed her hands over the shiny beads and crystals of the full skirt. "I bought it a few years ago when I was living with my ex-boyfriend. It was a whole long story, and I never told my fian—husband—the truth about it." She sighed. "It feels like bad luck to start a marriage this way."

"I don't believe in luck," Jay said.

"Are you married?" she asked, gesturing to his clasped hands.

"I am," he answered for the second time that evening. He lifted his hand and stupidly patted the gold band on his ring finger. "Two decades now."

"Wow," she said, no longer crying. "Do you still love her?"

Jay laughed and shuffled his feet, suddenly uneasy. "Yes, of course."

She sighed and brushed the tulle off her shoulder as if it were her hair. "My husband and me . . . we moved too fast. I'm scared there's too much we don't know about each other." Her voice cracked, and she dropped her chin to her chest. "I should've told him the truth about my dress and previous relationship. He's such a good person." She glanced at Jay. "His name is Eric. He's so hardworking and honest. Practically perfect."

"No one's perfect," Jay said. "And it's okay to not know *everything* about each other."

But was that true? Did Jay really believe that? He'd never kept any secrets from Tricia. None. A fact that used to make him feel proud, until the moment he'd looked through her bag and wondered, for the first time in their marriage, if she could say the same.

The bride sobbed, and Jay gently patted her on the back.

She lifted her head and looked at him. "Why am I like this?" she asked.

"Like what?"

"So secretive. Why can't I just tell the truth?" She gave him an imploring look. "What if he's keeping secrets from me, too?"

"I don't know," Jay said, and once again, the knowledge of that damn library book felt like a nagging splinter just beneath the surface of his skin. "Everyone does fucked up things sometimes."

The bride laughed, a half-sob, half-barking sound. She suddenly leaned over and kissed him, pressing her warm, tear-damp lips to the sides of his own. Stunned, Jay couldn't think, but his eyes instinctively closed and he didn't push her away. The kiss was soft and sweet. He couldn't remember the last time Tricia had kissed him like that.

The elevator dinged as the doors opened, and Jay quickly pulled away. Howard stood alone inside the carriage, staring at them. Jay's cheeks flooded with heat, and he lifted his hand to say something—what, he didn't know—but the doors closed, and the man disappeared.

"Oh, my God, I'm sorry," The bride said. She wiped her face and stood. She fluffed the large skirt of her dress and smoothed her veil once more. "I shouldn't have done that."

"It's okay," Jay said, though nothing about the last sixty seconds of his life felt okay.

"I should get back," she said.

"Yeah, me, too," Jay said.

She smiled sadly at him. "Thanks for sitting with me."

"Sure."

She pushed the elevator button, and within a few seconds, the doors opened. She got on and stood, still and serene, her beautiful designer gown with a French name perfectly fanned out around her.

"Maybe I'll tell him the truth about the dress someday," she said. Just as the doors started to close, she offered a small, final wave and was gone.

Jay remained seated, watching the digital numbers decrease as she rode down to the lobby to her reception, her waiting guests, and new husband, who didn't know some big secret about her wedding dress that had a name.

He couldn't help but wonder—if she told him, would they make it?

But what, really, did it mean for a couple to "make it"? Had he and Tricia "made it" yet? Would it not feel like they'd truly "made it" until one of them died, and the other could declare *until death do us part?*

Jay finally rose and started for the elevator, but changed his mind and took the stairs, climbing the three flights as fast as he could, breathless by the time he reached the sixth floor.

When he entered their dark room, all the suitcases were packed and lined up neatly by the door. Tricia sat on the edge of one bed, legs crossed, her workbag—with the mysterious children's book still inside—resting beside her as she scrolled through her phone. The girls sat next to each other on the opposite bed, faces aglow from their dying phone screens.

Of course, Tricia had taken care of getting their things in order again. He knew before he'd even opened the door that she'd be there waiting for him, ready to get on with it all.

Jar of Nails

What happened at the baby shower was inevitable, Jessie later realized. After all, the dentist had informed her just the day before that her teeth were showing evidence of grinding. Most adult grinders, he'd said, develop the habit as a response to stress. Was she experiencing an increased or unusual level of stress lately? Jessie had nodded, her chin crinkling the ill-fitting paper bib around her neck, tears springing to her eyes. "I'm having problems with my husband." And she had proceeded to spew the details of her and Dave's terrible fight. The dentist had uncomfortably cleared his throat, written her a prescription for a nighttime bite guard, and abruptly excused himself for a root canal emergency.

So, with her jaw clenched and still aching, she arrived at the Waterford Tea Room, a nineteenth-century bed and breakfast in the trendy section of downtown Minneapolis, for the baby shower. Even with several minutes to spare, she still had to park on the street and totter up the gravel drive with her spiked heels—normally saved for weddings or special dinner dates with her husband, but appropriate for this type of shower crowd—sinking into the soft spring ground. She carried a glittery pink bag containing a package of disposable diapers, wipes, lotion, and lavender organic soap. She knew the gifts were impersonal for a close friend, but by the time she'd gotten around to shopping, the Target store registry had been barren.

As Jessie slipped into the grand foyer, she looked for Kristy—the new mother—her friend since Minnesota State, where they'd met as business majors. Each had dated and later married a player on the university lacrosse team. They'd remained friends over the years, socializing occasionally, and eventually buying houses a few streets apart in the same suburban development. Even though their college-based friendship hadn't always worn well under the harsh lights of adulthood, Jessie still enjoyed Kristy's company and was genuinely happy about the baby.

"You made it."

Jessie turned and found herself face-to-face with Meredith, the hostess of the shower and one of Kristy's newer neighborhood friends.

"I'm not late, am I?" Jessie asked.

"No, no," Meredith waved, a graceful and controlled gesture. "We just weren't sure you'd come." She carefully brushed her glossy, dark hair from her shoulder.

Had it been anyone else, Jessie would have asked what she meant, but Meredith was still more of an acquaintance, and Jessie felt intimidated by her. Tall and slender, with insane cheekbones and great taste in everything, Meredith was a big-time social media influencer. Kristy talked about her constantly—*Meredith* says, *Meredith* does—and practically lived and died by Meredith's posts, which only made Jessie feel even more insecure around her.

"Let me take that for you," Meredith said, lifting the bag from Jessie's hand.

Jessie straightened the leather belt of her dress and moved the clasp of her necklace to the back of her neck, reminding herself to unclench her jaw. She followed Meredith into the formal tearoom, where the heavy Edwardian furniture had been decorated with clusters of fresh peonies in crystal vases, creating photo ops from multiple angles. A gourmet two-tier cake commanded the center of the refreshment table. The bottom tier, decorated in a realistic-looking row of toy blocks, spelled out the new baby's name. *Kahrlee.*

Shit. Jessie had spelled the name wrong on the card, even though she'd seen the correct spelling on the invitation. For a moment, she considered sneaking over to her gift to ditch the envelope with the offensive spelling, but Meredith was near the gifts, taking a selfie with another woman, and Jessie preferred to stay as far away from her as possible.

"Jess!" Kristy—bearing a small layer of pregnancy insulation around her middle but otherwise just as sweet and unchanged from their college days—approached and offered a light, single-armed hug while cradling the baby in the other.

Jessie folded back a corner of the pink blanket to get a closer look at the newborn, a pinched-faced girl with a large, misshapen head and lightly jaundiced skin. "Oh, she's so… tiny," she said, forcing a smile. "Congratulations."

"Thank you! She looks just like Chad, don't you think?" Kristy reached out to squeeze Jessie's hand. "I'm so glad you're here. Why don't you sit with Tricia? You remember Tricia from our housewarming party, right? She and her husband are the doctors who live in the giant house across the street from me and Meredith."

Kristy turned to greet another guest but still held tight to Jessie's hand, forcing Jessie to stand awkwardly at Kristy's side until she unceremoniously released it. Jessie inched her way through the crowd of chattering women, most of whom she didn't recognize, to an empty seat in the last row of chairs next to Tricia. Tricia, some ten years older than the other women in their neighborhood social circle, was a dermatologist married to an anesthesiologist. The only couple Jessie knew who'd had an actual live-in nanny when their girls were infants. Dave liked to joke that Tricia and her husband's dual "ologist" was from the Latin term meaning "more money than God," but Jessie always had to force herself to laugh at that joke.

"Jessie," Tricia said, moving her jacket from an empty seat next to her, "I'm so glad you decided to come. Seems like ages since we talked. How's the job going? Are you still at that business consulting place?"

Jessie sat and smoothed the hem of her dress. "Yes, I was just promoted to senior consultant."

Tricia, though friendly enough, also made Jessie nervous, but for reasons different than Meredith. Tricia was unfussy and practical, often wearing Birkenstock clogs for just about every occasion. But beneath that easygoing exterior, she was sharp and intense—sometimes making conversations feel more like interrogations.

"What's the promotion?" Tricia studied her face, leaning uncomfortably close so that Jessie could smell her breath—coffee and possibly something onion-y from lunch.

"Well, I'm still involved in marketing consultations and rebranding for struggling companies and organizations." Jessie hated the way her explanation always sounded—like she was reading her job description off a cheesy brochure. "Only now I oversee a team of consultants. It's a lot more responsibility, but I'm enjoying the challenge and—"

"I always say it's good to be someone's boss," Tricia said with a congratulatory pat to Jessie's knee, then turned away to say something to a woman who sat down on her other side.

Jessie was relieved. She was too emotionally drained to deal with a baby shower *and* a conversation with Tricia.

From the front of the room, Meredith clapped her hands. "Ladies, let's start the game. Seven diapers, each with a different melted candy bar inside, will be passed around. The object is to guess the name of the candy bar. You're allowed to smell, touch, and taste."

"Oh, I love a good contest!" Kristy said, and Jessie couldn't help but think of the long-ago college night at Sharkey's

Bar when Kristy had entered a wet T-shirt contest and was awarded a free pitcher of beer for second place, losing to a girl with much smaller breasts but who had flashed the crowd.

"God," Tricia said under her breath. "I hate these stupid games. What is it with all you Midwesterners and lame baby shower games? Chocolate-shit diapers, so tacky. I would've expected something a little more tasteful from Meredith. She's from Connecticut, for Christ's sake."

"I'm from the Midwest and never played this one," Jessie said. She inspected the first diaper handed to her and made a face. "I agree. It's kind of a disgusting game."

"My sister-in-law did it at my baby shower, so you *know* it has to be moronic," Tricia said, handing a second diaper to Jessie without even a glance at the contents. "By the way," she hoisted an enormous handbag onto her lap, "I know it's, like, *taboo*, to talk to other women about this, but I don't care. I'm giving you the name of a fertility guy. I'll text it to you." She retrieved her phone.

Jessie shook her head. "Fertility guy?"

"Yeah, a specialist I know who helped me and Jay, and Meredith and Mike get pregnant. Dave told Jay you're having trouble."

Jessie stared at Tricia and swallowed hard, unsure how she'd sound when she opened her mouth to speak. "Dave said that we're having trouble getting pregnant?"

"Yeah, he mentioned it while all the guys were playing golf the other day. Just in passing, so don't be pissed at him. Jay said he seemed upset."

Jessie sat back in her chair and dropped her hands into the chocolate shit.

Tricia started typing on her phone "Dr. Glowackie," she said. "Terrible name. Great doc. Been around forever."

Jessie's phone dinged with the shared contact. She opened the screen and read the text. *Dr. James J. Glowackie, M.D., F.A.C.O.G.*

As her trembling fingers left a chocolate smudge on the screen, she thought about the jar of nails.

Shortly after college graduation, Jessie and Dave had dismantled his homemade loft bed in his tiny fraternity house bedroom; they had pried the haphazardly assembled boards apart and dropped the nails into an empty box. The box was filled to the brim with nails by the time the job was finished, and Dave had inexplicably kept the box after the move.

Then, after they got married and settled comfortably into their new apartment, Dave brought out the box and placed it on a bathroom shelf, where it sat behind the extra rolls of toilet paper. He decided it would be funny if they used the nails in a humorous spin on the old "put a penny in a jar every time you have sex the first year of marriage, take one out every time after the first year, and you'll never get to the bottom of the jar." Get it? Nails? Dave had laughed and Jessie had too, because they'd always shared a weird, rather perverted sense of humor, one of the things she loved most about him.

For the first year, they'd faithfully taken a nail from the box and placed it in an empty glass pickle jar on top of their bureau, a jar that rapidly filled. Then, after their first anniversary, they'd faithfully removed a nail from the pickle jar, laughing at how the rate of nails slowed, just like the old saying. By year three, it was even slower when Dave lost his IT job and was out of work for several months, and then the next year when Jessie's sister lived with them during an internship. Nevertheless, the supply was slowly but surely diminishing. And what the hell, Dave said, once they emptied the jar, they'd start trying to have a baby. Let the nails decide!

Again, Jessie had laughed and agreed because it was such a "Dave and Jessie thing" to do.

Last fall, around the time they'd purchased the new house just five streets away from Kristy, in the same neighborhood as Tricia and Meredith, the nails in the jar were down to a half dozen, and Dave, with his usual mixture of humor and seriousness, saw the timing as a sign, just like he'd said. What does it mean when we buy a bigger house in the right neighborhood at the same time we get down to our last dozen nails? Diaphragm burning ceremony! he'd proclaimed to the slightly drunken laughter of Jessie and their dinner guests. We'll then use the nails to build this kid a loft when he goes off to college! It'll become a goddamn family legacy! And Jessie and their friends all knew that was exactly what he would do, and the story told over wine and prime rib was perfectly offbeat and charming, just like Dave.

Then two months ago, they'd gotten down to their last nail, and suddenly Jessie stopped laughing. The last nail had remained there since, in the jar, lonely and abandoned.

"You know," Tricia said, "I didn't go to baby showers for years when I was trying to get pregnant. It was just too brutal." She thrust another diaper into Jessie's face. "Ugh. I can't figure this one out. It smells like a Kit Kat, but it looks too smooth."

Jessie stared down at the chocolate smear.

One morning, two months ago, she'd gone to the bureau for a pair of underwear and had looked up to see the last nail in the jar. Suddenly, she couldn't breathe. She had felt a subtle tightening in her chest for some time as the nail supply had depleted, but standing in front of the glass jar and facing down the reality of the last nail, the tightness intensified painfully and terrified her.

"I don't know what it is either," Jessie said to Tricia. She passed the diaper to the woman on her left.

The change had been instantaneous. She'd become restless and edgy, snapping at Dave over the way he parked the car in the garage, the way he spit toothpaste all over the bathroom faucet, how he buttered his toast on the kitchen counter without a plate and left a trail of crumbs that would surely track from one end of the house to the other. She started working late on a project that wasn't due for months. Dave noticed the change in her and asked what was wrong, what was bothering her—nothing, *nothing*, she kept telling him. Everything is fine. But she'd stopped having sex with him, claiming she was too tired, too stressed. He'd noticed that too, of course, and asked if she was having an affair. Of course not! she'd vehemently proclaimed, and the last nail remained in the jar.

Finally, during a terrible fight a few days before her dental appointment, she had said the words that made Dave's face turn pale and his lips slowly part in disbelief. Or despair.

I don't know if I want a baby.

He had slumped onto the couch. It's a big step, he'd said in a hoarse voice, it could be nerves or fear, that's natural. Maybe you just don't want one right now.

No! she'd wanted to scream. I don't want one ever! And maybe I've never wanted one but ignored it because I figured my feelings would eventually change because you're my best friend, but here we are, and my feelings haven't changed, and I still don't want one. I could be happy with just the two of us, and I'm so sorry, I'm so fucking sorry!

But she couldn't bring herself to say any of it because as long as she was just *unsure*—just nervous, like Dave said—she could pretend she hadn't had one of the cruelest changes of heart that could occur in a marriage, and she desperately didn't want to be *that* person in her marriage.

So there she was, just one day after the dentist had asked her if she had been grinding her teeth because of stress, at a goddamn baby shower holding chocolate-shit diapers while everyone around her thought she was having trouble getting pregnant because that's what her husband told them, because it was, in Dave's mind, a smaller but less painful version of the truth.

"Jess! It's your turn to hold Kahrlee!" Kristy said, materializing with her enormous milk-swollen breasts that would handily sweep first place in any wet T-shirt contest now.

Jessie pushed her chair back, the scraping sound of wood against wood quickly swept up by the high ceilings of the room. "Oh, no, really, I—"

"Seriously, Kristy," Tricia said, sitting up straighter and putting her hand out as if directing traffic. "She doesn't want to hold the baby. Give her a break."

"Oh, I think it would be good for her." Kristy leaned down with little Kahrlee bundled in her outstretched arms. She shifted the pink fleece bundle from the crook of her arm into Jessie's. As Jessie scrambled to set her phone down and swipe her sticky fingers on her skirt, Baby Kahrlee, the pink fleecy bundle, to her horror, slipped through her arms and down her legs, like a child descending a playground chute, sliding soundlessly to the floor.

Jessie's hands flew to her mouth. Gasps. Chatter stopped. Silverware ceased its tinny scrape across plates. Every woman in the room, sitting nearby or standing next to the cake or lingering by the door hoping to catch a light breeze, froze.

Kahrlee let out a healthy, screeching wail as Kristy snatched up the tightly bundled little body and clutched her to her chest. "Fuck!" she shrieked. "Kahrlee! Oh, my God!"

Within seconds, every woman descended upon Kristy and the howling baby, producing cell phones to call for an ambulance, search the nearest hospital, and even a moment of prayer from someone in the back. Jessie stood, her hands still clamped to her mouth, and backed away as a few women patted her shoulders, murmuring, it's okay, it could have happened to anyone, it was an accident.

"Everyone, calm down!" Tricia shouted. "I'm a doctor." She scooped Kahrlee out of Kristy's arms and set her on the massive walnut sideboard, where she quickly unwrapped the pink blanket. Kahrlee, no longer wailing, whimpered and kicked her pudgy legs in the air and attempted to stick her fist in her mouth. Tricia carefully prodded her fingers over every inch of her head, neck, back, arms, and legs. She removed a doctor's pen light from her bottomless purse (Jessie had seen her produce the same light at Kristy's housewarming party for a man who passed out after too many dirty martinis) and shone it into Kahrlee's squinty eyes.

Kristy hovered at Tricia's elbow, clutching a napkin Meredith had handed to her while she stood with her arm wrapped tightly around Kristy's shoulders.

Tricia straightened after a few moments. "Kristy," she said, "the baby's unhurt."

"Oh, thank you, Lord!" Kristy cried, and a few women clapped.

"She was so tightly swaddled in that thick blanket," Tricia said, "you probably could've tossed her down a flight of stairs and she would've been fine." She snorted but stopped quickly when no one joined her. "You can take her to your pediatrician for a quick check if you want, but seriously, she's okay."

Jessie finally stepped forward. "Kristy," she said, her voice hoarse and trembling. "I am so, so sorry. I, I don't know what happened."

Kristy lifted the baby from the table and pressed her cheek to Kahrlee's downy hair-covered head. "She's not hurt. That's all that matters."

"I'm just mortified," Jessie continued. "I really can't tell you how sorry I am."

Kristy swiped her nose with the napkin. "It's okay, Jess, really. It was an accident. I shouldn't have tried to force you to hold her with everything you're going through."

"Could've happened to anyone," Tricia said, replacing the light in her bag. "Babies get dropped more often than you'd think."

The crowd began to disperse, and a few women returned to their seats, while others wandered to the cake table to sample refreshments, many rehashing baby-dropping stories of their own.

Jessie slipped out of the tearoom, her purse clutched to her chest, and scurried toward the powder room. Tears burned her eyes, and she could no longer stop them. Only now she wasn't crying because she had dropped Kristy's baby. She was crying because she knew she would have to say it out loud to Dave—there was no *unsure*, there was no *nervous*. She didn't ever want a child.

Jessie opened the bathroom door and was startled to find Meredith inside, sitting on the closed lid of the toilet, smoking a cigarette.

"Shut the door," Meredith hissed.

Jessie whisked the door shut and then briefly wondered if Meredith had meant for her to *leave* and close the door behind her. Regardless, she slumped against the floral-papered wall and the tears flowed freely, running down her cheeks, dripping off her chin, staining the light satin fabric of her dress.

"Stop crying, Jessie." Meredith lifted the lid of the toilet and tossed in her cigarette, where it sizzled. "That," she said, looking at Jessie, "is the ugliest baby I've seen in my life, even before you dropped it."

#targetdown

Kristy pushed the red shopping cart into the redolent candle aisle and stopped to re-tuck sleeping Kahrlee's pink and yellow duck blanket when the baby momentarily squirmed inside her infant seat from the cart basket. Her stomach fluttered with so much anticipation that her mouth nearly spread into a stupid, childish grin.

But she needed to focus. Needed to keep her face neutral.

Once Kahrlee was resettled and contentedly sucking on her pacifier, Kristy began strolling again, zeroing in on the shelves of colorful glass jars that smelled like delicious foods and summery floral bouquets. The cart glided silently over the polished tile floor as if rolling across glass, a sensation so pleasurable it made her cheeks and neck flush. Target store carts were the best. Large, clean, and the perfect height.

Despite her excited flush, the skin of Kristy's bare arms and legs pimpled in the cool air. She wished she'd thought to bring a light cardigan to wear over her loose shift dress. And she hated this dress—baggy and dumpy on her—but she still couldn't fit into her pre-pregnancy summer clothes even though it had been three months since she'd given birth. Everything in her life felt ill-fitting most days, except for her weekly trips to Target.

Kristy stopped in front of a new candle scent called "Salty Air" her friend Meredith had mentioned just yesterday on her social media. She opened her phone screen and double-checked Meredith's story one more time.

Meredith McCombs mizmeredesigns ✓
#saltyair Perfect scent for the start of summer! #ambiance #candles #thankyouWhimsyWicks
June 15

Kristy pinched and expanded the attached photo to study the composition. It was taken on Meredith's three-season porch; Kristy knew by the enormous white canvas sectional in the background. The twenty-nine-dollar, three-wick, cinereal-colored candle glowed next to a porcelain bowl of clipped fern fronds and an old-fashioned white pitcher of fresh lavender, perfectly situated in the center of her teak coffee table. Over twelve thousand hearts.

Kristy picked up the "Salty Air" candle and held it against her chest for a moment, then with a deliberate look of calm, pushed the cart out of the candle aisle and into the kitchen section. With the candle still clutched in one hand, she studied the wall of utensils, selecting a spatula, a slotted spoon, and a whisk, dramatically juggling the items in her hands as if struggling to make a critical decision.

She discreetly glanced around to ensure no one was nearby, adjusted her body so that her back was now square to the nearest security camera in the ceiling, and bumped the shopping cart hard with her hip. Kahrlee startled awake, spit out her pacifier, and began to writhe and kvetch in her car carrier, finally emitting a series of ear-splitting screeches. Kristy leaned over the cart and set the items down on Kahrlee's legs to adjust the duck blanket around her in the car seat. As she did this, she pulled a corner of the blanket over the candle in a swift, nearly imperceptible motion, nestling it deep into the seat on the side of Kahrlee's tiny body.

Kristy half-heartedly shushed the baby and rolled the cart back and forth for a moment as the previous belly butterflies now turned to rippled thrills. She loved that feeling. A cross between excitement and danger. Like having sex in a public place. As Kahrlee continued to cry, she calmly put the three kitchen utensils back on their respective hooks, and rubbed her temples in a show of Frazzled New Mother in case anyone was now watching. She steered the cart toward the registers.

She had perfected the routine with five critical steps to success:

1. Shop at five p.m. during the busiest time of day when employees were most distracted by other customers.

2. Identify locations of all nearby security cameras.

3. Watch and wait for empty aisles.

4. Create a distraction with multiple items, a fussy baby, and use sleight of hand.

5. Include name-brand necessities in cart, like diapers and formula (necessities justified the shopping trip, and name brands showed she had money).

6. Check out with said fussy baby (the louder the cries the better).

7. Always use regular checkout (not self-checkouts because they were more closely monitored by employees) and look frazzled for cashiers so they would hurry along the checkout process.

Today, she'd smoothly executed five of the seven steps. Just two more to go, but they were arguably the most precarious.

At the front of the store, Kristy was surprised to find unusually long lines streaming from every cashier's lane and even the self-checkout area. Kristy selected the shortest line closest to the doors—still four people deep—and stopped behind a woman with a full cart to wait her turn. As if on cue, Kahrlee's wails hit a crescendo. Right about this time was when someone usually took pity on her and let her cut the line, thus getting her out of the store faster, but today, no one offered.

Kristy rolled the cart back and forth making soothing noises, still hoping someone would tire of the incessant wails and let her jump ahead. She opened her phone to read a social media notification. Meredith had made a new post about an expensive hair cream her stylist had sent her to try. Meredith, it seemed, never paid for anything anymore. As a legitimate influencer, her 120K followers ensured a steady stream of freebies.

Free hand lotion and makeup don't pay the bills, Chad constantly told Kristy when she complained about it, her voice always thick with childish envy. She knew what Chad said was true, and yet she still couldn't help but get sucked into Meredith's social media vortex every single day, feeling like maybe if she had a beautiful "Salty Air" candle like Meredith, or a twenty-dollar bag of designer coffee, or an expensive bottle of hair cream, her life would somehow, magically, be "right."

Kristy glanced up from her phone when Kahrlee unleashed a particularly angry squawk and sighed irritably that the line hadn't moved yet.

The woman in front of her turned around. "I think something's wrong with the registers," she said. "Otherwise, I'd let you go ahead of me, you poor thing."

"Oh," Kristy replied, now noticing several Target employees hovering around the registers and kiosks, stabbing the screens with their fingers. "Thanks, anyway."

A brief tinge of nervousness crept up the back of her neck. She checked another social media app and spotted the hashtag *#targetdown* trending, with locations pinging in multiple cities and states.

"I think it might be widespread," Kristy said to the woman. "Like, more than just this store."

"Great," the woman muttered, leaning on her cart handle.

"Hey!" A man at the front of their line shouted at one of the young employees struggling with a computer. "How long is this going to take?"

"Sorry," The employee said. Her nametag read *Bilan*. "We're doing everything we can." She hunched toward the computer monitor again, squinting, and one of her long, beautifully beaded braids slipped over her shoulder and skimmed the keyboard.

The man scoffed and dropped his red basket on the ground with a loud slap.

Another social media notification popped up on Kristy's phone screen. A new post from Meredith.

Meredith McCombs @mizmeredesigns ✓ 1 min
Checkout lines backing up at Target w/ no registers working #targetdown

Meredith was at the Eden Prairie Target near their neighborhood, while Kristy was at the Minnehaha Center because she never used the Target near her house when she planned to sponge.

That's what she mentally called it. Sponging. It felt like a less terrible word than what she was actually doing. Like less of a crime, an actual misdemeanor.

Kristy had started sponging back in high school because one of her friends did it, and it was kind of fun and felt dangerously cool at the time. But she'd kept doing it long after the friendship ended and Kristy went away to college and was stressed by classes, money, boyfriends, and figuring life out. It gave her relief when everything felt wrong and confusing, and she'd quickly become addicted, like a heroin addict. Sponging always cheered her up, when everything else in her life felt like shit.

But once she got a full-time job after college as a software analyst and started making real money, she stopped doing it. She'd married Chad, and they built a nice life together with two incomes. When she became pregnant with Kahrlee, they bought a house in the suburbs, and Kristy swapped out Software Analysis for Stay-At-Home Mother, which felt like the "right" thing to do.

Only, from the beginning, nothing about motherhood felt "right." Once again, everything in her life felt like shit.

And so here she was, back to her old sponging habit.

More minutes passed. Every line at the checkouts grew longer, ballooning to ten, fifteen, twenty people deep. Customers fidgeted; their increasing irritation was palpable.

Kristy felt her previous flush of adrenaline and excitement, that brief feeling of "right," slowly erode to worry.

What did that word even mean, "right"? The right way to parent, the right way to love, the right way to live. Kristy didn't know anymore. Everything felt wrong, like *shit*, but Kristy didn't know how to go back and undo it all, or rather *re*-do it all and possibly find a new version of what "right" might look like for her. She felt stuck and wrong, and the beautiful Merediths of the world—with their perfect children and husbands and cultivated social media accounts and thousands of devoted followers—only further twisted and beat her joints painfully out of shape until she no longer recognized her contorted self.

Kahrlee continued to fuss and kick her legs, wadding up the blanket around her feet, uncovering the candle. Once Kristy noticed, a jolt of panic zipping through her gut. She hastily tucked it back around Kahrlee's body. She checked to ensure no one had seen the hidden candle, but everyone around her, save the loud man at the front of her line, was thankfully staring at their phone screens.

The man snapped his fingers at another Target employee, shouting, "Hey! Hey!" but to no avail.

"It's not their fault," The woman in front of Kristy said to him. "All the Target systems are down everywhere. I read it on the internet."

"Well, I really need this for my wife," he said, holding up a six-pack of Diet Pepsi bottles.

"Then go down the street to CVS and buy it," the woman said. "Why are you waiting in line here? That isn't an essential item."

The man's jaw clenched as he moved toward her. "Oh, really?" he said, rifling through her cart. "And what about you?" He held up a bag of Tostitos. "Is this essential, too?"

She snatched the bag out of his hand. "Don't touch my things!"

"They're not 'your things,' lady." He made a pair of exaggerated air quotes close to her face. "You haven't even paid for them yet!"

Kristy focused on Kahrlee and not the ratcheting scene before her. She dabbed nonexistent spit up from the baby's chin. People behind her rustled and murmured as the pair continued arguing.

Suddenly, the woman pivoted and grabbed the package of diapers from Kristy's cart.

"See?!" she shouted now. "Other people *are* in line for essentials! And the rest of us with nonessentials aren't complaining!"

"Please don't involve me," Kristy said, gently extracting the diapers from the woman's hands.

"I'm not," The woman snapped, her ire quickly transferring. "I'm making a point."

"What point?" The man shouted, his face flushing. "That you're sticking your damn nose into everyone else's business where it doesn't belong?"

"Don't talk to me like that!" The woman shouted back.

"Jesus, people," the young man behind Kristy said. "It's turned Darwinian in here."

A teenage girl behind him discreetly pointed her phone at the arguing pair, recording, no doubt.

An itchy rivulet of perspiration rolled down the center of Kristy's back. Kahrlee was full-on bawling now, her entire head turning an angry, splotchy crimson, making her infant acne pop across her face. She violently thrashed her legs, and Kristy fought to keep the blanket secured over the item stashed in the crevice of the carrier.

"See what you've done?" The woman said, pointing at Kristy and the baby.

Kristy tried desperately to soothe Kahrlee with her pacifier, but Kahrlee wailed louder and turned her head away, her tiny, clenched fists punching the air.

"Shh, shh, it's okay, it's okay, sweetie," Kristy said, stupidly shaking a plastic rattle in Kahrlee's face, which only enraged the baby further. Kristy kept her other hand firmly on the corner of the blanket. If she picked Kahrlee up, the sponged items could be exposed with everyone watching her now.

The woman turned back around. "Aww, poor thing. Can I try to hold her?"

"No!" Kristy paused to collect herself. "I'm sorry, no, thank you. She's, she's very afraid of strangers."

The woman eyed Kristy. "Suit yourself."

Bilan approached the line again, looking terrified and about to cry right alongside Kahrlee. "We're so sorry," she said, twisting the bullseye pin above her name on the tag. "We're having, like, some kind of system issue affecting all our software. We're trying to figure out how to get you checked out if you want to, like, stay and wait. Otherwise, our manager said to bring your cart over there." She gestured to a woman at the doors, checking the items in everyone's carts. "We'll make a list of all your items and put your name on it so that you can come back later when everything is fixed."

Acidic panic swelled from the pit of Kristy's stomach and lodged itself sickeningly in the back of her throat. Kahrlee kicked and punched the air even harder now, and Kristy wrestled to keep the blanket in place.

Even if she left her cart now, it was too risky to try and get the carrier out of the cart and through the door with a manager standing right there, checking everything and everyone.

"This is ridiculous," the man said. "I'm not coming back to this store or any of your stores ever again." He stalked to the exit and disappeared through the sliding doors.

"Good riddance," the woman said.

Bilan wrung her hands and said, straining to raise her voice over Kahrlee's wails, "We apologize for the inconvenience."

Another customer behind Kristy abruptly set her two items on a shelf near the checkout and left. Kristy's phone dinged again with more social media notifications, one after another, but Kristy felt too paralyzed to even pick it up. She needed to go somewhere else in the store to get the candle out of the car seat and get the hell out of there. Her toes, exposed in a pair of cheap flip flops, had gone numb from the cold air conditioning and turned an abnormal white color. Kahrlee had cried so hard she was nearly hoarse.

Kristy steered her cart out of the line and pushed it into the nearby shoe section, which was empty of people and had a blind spot for the security cameras near the wall with hanging pairs of slippers. There, she removed the blanket and carefully unbuckled Kahrlee. As she lifted her out, the candle rolled into the pit of the seat. She held Kahrlee to her shoulder and began to gently sway back and forth while making gentle *shushing* noises.

After a few minutes, Kahrlee's cries lessened until she was silent but for a few intermittent sobs and sighs, and Kristy felt her own anxiety begin to ebb. She hadn't been that close to getting caught since high school when a security guard chased her out of a Younkers store with an eighty-dollar Calvin Klein blouse stuffed into her backpack.

Kristy's phone continued to ding with notifications, so she picked it up, unable to resist that noise like a Pavlovian dog.

Meredith had made another social media post a few minutes ago, and it was blowing up.

Meredith McCombs @mizmeredesigns ✔ 5 min
SERIOUSLY @Target registers down nearly 30 min and now telling us to leave baskets and carts with our names on them to come back and pay later?! Unacceptable. I shouldn't have to take time out of my busy day to come back. How are you going to make this right with me? #targetdown #targetfail

Comment after comment appeared.

@mizmeredesigns identified the true urban crisis. @Target checkouts are down nationwide and we're all going to die here #targetdown

@mizmeredesigns Wow why are you acting so awful about this? #targetdown

@mizmeredesigns don't you get all kinds of free shit from @Target as an influencer?

SERIOUSLY KAREN @mizmeredesigns

what a bitch @mizmeredesigns

@mizmeredesigns Dogs and cats living together it's mass hysteria! TARGETGEDDON

And here I thought being stuck in this @Target line during the outage with a wild toddler was the 7th circle of hell but clearly it's being stuck with @mizmeredesigns during #targetdown

This just in: @mizmeredesigns now rebranding as @mizmereentitlement

Meredith's follower numbers across all her social media accounts were dropping by the hundreds right before Kristy's eyes. Amid the shelves of summer slingbacks, Kristy watched open-mouthed the epic downfall of her friend-not-friend in real time.

But after several minutes, the comments turned nastier.

Entitled people like @mizmeredesigns should rid themselves of this world

Shorten the @Target lines for the rest of us

@Target @mizmeredesigns Someone shut this stupid bitch down

@mizmeredesigns just kill urself and spare the rest of us

@mizmeredesigns shut the fuck up or I'll shut you up

Kristy closed the app. She didn't want to watch the ugliness anymore. She put her phone away and let out a long, deep breath. Kahrlee now slept peacefully on her shoulder, her little body warm and heavy, and Kristy kept swaying and breathing until her arms began to tremble and ache.

A new sense of calm descended over her for the first time since Kahrlee was born.

They'd both emotionally exhausted themselves, it seemed.

Kristy pulled the blanket off the car seat and picked up the candle. She held the glass jar to her nose and closed her eyes, inhaling the pretty, summery scent one last time. Then, she put the jar in her car basket next to the package of diapers.

She carefully laid Kahrlee back down in the empty car seat, buckled her in, and hoisted the carrier with the handle over her forearm. She spotted the Target employee, Bilan, passing by the fitting rooms.

"Excuse me," Kristy said.

Bilan paused.

"I'm so sorry," Kristy continued, "but I don't want these items anymore. Is there somewhere I can leave them?" Bilan glanced at the items in the cart, at the candle that had, moments earlier, nearly and completely derailed Kristy's life.

"Sorry," Bilan said with a shrug, "but I just quit." And with that, she pulled her nametag off her shirt and dropped it into Kristy's cart.

Kristy smiled at her. "Good for you. Me, too."

Bilan smiled back and continued toward the front of the store.

Kristy slung her diaper bag over her shoulder and followed, past the candle aisle and the crowded checkout lanes where people were still waiting and complaining and staring at their phones, past the manager posted at the door to check saved items in everyone's carts, and crossed the threshold of the exit, through the automatic doors, and into the bright light of the warm summer day.

Spirit Babies

It could be said the global outage of Target store registers one hot June day triggered Meredith's simultaneous career and marriage implosion, but really, it was a routine medical question four years earlier that first spoiled the broth, as her grandmother used to say.

When she entered the superstore, she was armed with a short but specific list of items. Kitchen trash bags, a box of tampons, a greeting card, as well as a gift set of coconut and warm vanilla bath bombs, shower gel, and lotion—the latter being the most important item and only available at Target. She was utterly annoyed with herself since she'd just been there last week to pick up a new free candle she was asked to promote and had forgotten to get the other items. Then she got busy with other things and before she knew it, she'd nearly waited too long to get the gift and would have to mail it as soon as she left the store in order for it to arrive in Connecticut on Azlyn's birthday.

Azlyn. Even after four years, the name still felt buzzy and strange on her tongue. She'd only recently started to try out her nickname, Azzie, in an attempt to forge intimacy with the girl, but she wasn't quite there yet.

Inside the store, she started with the greeting card, quickly scanning the "Birthday for Her" section. She wanted something loving but not overly effusive, pretty but not gaudy, fun but not too childish for a nineteen-year-old college freshman.

Happy birthday! What a joy it's been to watch you grow up!

No. Inaccurate. She and Mike didn't actually raise her.

Birthday greetings to a lovely young woman

No. Too stiff and formal.

For our favorite birthday girl

No. Too juvenile. Also inaccurate.

Meredith kept searching, pulling one card, sliding it back into a slot, then another. And another.

Where was a card that said, *Hey, happy birthday, I know this is still awkward between you and me, but I'm trying.*

Finally, she found a card with a pretty but subtle heart and flower illustration that said,

Happy birthday to someone very special

And the interior text worked:

What a joy it is to have you in our lives

A little formal, but good enough.

She dropped the card and envelope into the red basket hooked over her arm and hurried across the store to the grocery section. There, she easily located her brand of trash bags since she knew the layout of that store as well as the Botox-ed lines of her own face. Next, she efficiently crossed a main aisle to the health section for the tampons, making up the time she'd wasted searching for a card, then jumped over two aisles to the beauty section.

She scanned the shelves of bath bombs, lotions, scrubs, and shower gels, discovering that the gift sets were annoyingly sprinkled throughout instead of stocked in a central location.

Tree Hut. No.

Eos. No.

Beloved. No.

All the wrong brands.

A visibly pregnant woman pushed her cart into the aisle and stopped just short of bumping into Meredith's hip with it. She shot the woman an icy glance, but the woman didn't notice as she browsed bottles of coconut oil lotions, probably for stretch marks erupting across her growing belly.

Where the hell was this gift set? A mild panic stirred in Meredith's chest at the thought the store might not have it in stock. She didn't have time to drive to another location.

The panic was quickly replaced by a flash of anger that made Meredith sweat beneath her armpits. Anger at Mike that she was always the one to stress and worry over gifts for Azlyn—Azzie—whatever, and nearly kill herself to get them wrapped and in the mail in time to arrive for the next important event. Christmas. Valentine's Day. Easter. Graduation. Birthday.

Meredith's phone softly dinged, and she glanced at the notification. A nail polish startup had tagged her @mizmere-designs account, asking her to try their line and (hopefully) promote it. She quickly sent a response with her info where they could mail the samples.

She sighed and returned to her search, hot anger drilling down from her chest deep into her gut.

The pregnant woman selected a bottle of coconut lotion Meredith knew wouldn't help and dropped it into her cart. Meredith rolled her eyes at the wasted money, but the flash of judge-y annoyance was unexpectedly replaced with a hard lump in her throat from the threat of tears. Her eyes watered, making the colorful labels swim in front of her. Even now, the sight of a pregnant woman sometimes still filled her with sadness and envy.

Despite having sweet little Maya almost three years ago, the raw pain of struggling to conceive her never quite went away.

Maya. Meredith's Spirit Baby. Like the book said. *Spirit Babies: Communicating with the child you're meant to have.*

A book her neighbor Tricia had given her along with the name of the best fertility doctor in the city, Dr. Glowackie. Terrible name, great doc.

Only Maya technically wasn't their first Spirit Baby. Azlyn was, wasn't she?

Meredith had learned about the existence of another possible Spirit Baby at an appointment with Dr. Glowackie one Tuesday afternoon.

Have you gotten anyone pregnant before?

Mike's concerning pause.

"Um . . . well . . ."

Full alarm then. Meredith had practically given herself whiplash when she snapped her head to look at him.

Mike stared down at his hands. "Um," he said again, quietly. "Yes."

Meredith didn't know why, but she'd laughed. Or more like guffawed. The only time in her life she'd made that kind of bursting noise—part laugh, part snort, part choking—and said, "Really." A hard statement, no question.

"In high school," Mike answered. "I was seventeen. A senior. She was a year younger."

She glanced at Dr. Glowackie, but he was writing on his notepad, utterly unmoved by this ground-shifting admission.

"So, what," Meredith said, "did she have an abortion or something?"

"Yeah, mmm-hmm," Mike answered. "She had an abortion."

"Well." She'd taken a deep breath and gripped the armrests to keep from driving her fists through the windows. "At least we now know our inability to get pregnant is all my fault."

In the store, Meredith finally spotted the gift set on the top shelf: the Earth Goddess vegan brand Azlyn had specifically requested. She dropped the box into the basket and hurried to the checkout lanes. If she could get through check out and to her car in under five minutes or less, she would make it to the post office with almost ten minutes to spare. Just enough time to wrap, box, and priority rush the gift.

The line at the self-checkout kiosks was too long, so she selected a lane with a cashier finishing up with a customer.

As Meredith waited, she read the greeting card one more time with a twinge of doubt.

What a joy it is to have you in our lives.

She put it back it in the basket. Not enough time to search for another one.

But was the card true? Was it a joy to have Azlyn in their lives?

It certainly was for Mike. And his parents. Even Maya adored her older sister. Like a fun aunt who occasionally showed up to take her to the pool, or out for ice cream.

For Meredith, though, it was still . . . a process.

Learning Mike's high school pregnancy admission had been the shocking first part of the process, but okay, Meredith had understood Mike's reasons for never telling her. They moved on. Focused once more on communicating with *their* Spirit Baby. Making their Spirit Baby a Real Baby.

But one night, two weeks later, they'd just gone to bed and switched off their nightlights when Mike had sighed heavily, and said, "Mere, I have to tell you something."

Thus began the second part of the process. Learning there was no abortion. The former girlfriend from high school, Tiffany, had decided to have and keep the baby. And her family had asked Mike to sign papers giving away his rights, promising he'd have nothing to do with the child. He'd agreed. He'd already planned to attend college three hours away, had paid tuition, found a roommate, and had a job lined up. In his stupid, eighteen-year-old mind it was just easier not to tell anyone, sign away his rights, and move on. The next fall, he heard through friends, Tiffany had given birth to a baby girl.

Lying in bed that night, Meredith learned there was, to her silent devastation, already a Spirit Baby in the world with Mike's distinct blue eyes, and her name was Azlyn.

"And I want to meet her," he said. "My Spirit Baby. I've missed too much of her life."

Part three of the process: meeting her husband's fifteen-year-old daughter, the girl's mother, adopted father, and highly disapproving grandparents all in one shot. Overnight, Meredith became a stepmother in the midst of her desperate quest to become an actual mother. Or real mother? Or natural mother? She never knew how to distinguish between the two.

"Stepmother" was such an unsettling role because Meredith had hated her own stepmother, a woman who acted like a jealous toddler whenever Meredith's father gave her any attention. The joke was on her, though, when Meredith found herself internally seething with envy over Mike's newly divided priorities, and she kept finishing in second place.

So, she overcompensated to cover her ridiculous feelings. She planned special vacations with Azlyn, FaceTime calls, group texts, and buying all the thoughtful gifts. Beautifully wrapped, with a loving card, and mailed in plenty of time for the birthday or holiday.

Less than a year after meeting Azlyn, Meredith finally had Maya, *her* Spirit Baby. But Maya's addition to their family didn't feel as big as Azlyn's. Everyone was trying to make up for lost time with her, and Maya's arrival had felt mundane in comparison. Commonplace. Though Meredith never said anything, it nearly burned her alive. But she kept planning the trips, FaceTime calls, buying the gifts, mailing them on time. Taking care of her second-place Spirit Baby. Building a social media career with candles and throw pillows and blankets and wall décor because it filled the time.

In the checkout lane, Meredith unloaded her items onto the conveyor belt. She removed her wallet from her purse, ready to swipe her card.

The cashier, a young man, attempted to scan her first item—the trash bags—but frowned. He tried again, squinting at his computer screen.

"Uh, something is . . ." He pecked random keys on the keyboard, then tried to scan the tampons instead.

The cashier in the lane next to him turned and said, "Hey. My computer isn't working."

"Yeah," he said. "Mine isn't either."

Meredith glanced at the clock on her phone and felt a small uptick in her heart rate. "Can't you just restart it?" she asked.

"Umm, well . . . I don't . . . know." More pecking at keys until Meredith wanted to reach across the conveyor belt and break them. Snap each and every bone in half.

Other employees appeared like mirages around the registers. Managers, Meredith could see on their nametags. Good. Get your asses out here and fix this.

She checked her phone screen again. The time cushion for the post office was dwindling.

One of the assistant managers squeezed behind the register and immediately apologized for the inconvenience. More key pecking even Meredith could clearly see was useless by the frozen screen on the monitor.

She impatiently tapped the edge of her card on the lean pad. She opened a social media site on her phone and started scrolling. Sure enough, a hashtag was already trending from multiple locations around the country. *#targetdown*

Behind her, a line grew into the clothing section with restless customers murmuring complaints beneath their breath.

Meredith quickly typed a post.

Meredith McCombs @mizmeredesigns ✔
Checkout lines backing up at Target w/ no registers working #targetdown

Now the assistant manager was on his cell phone. With each passing minute, the muscles in Meredith's face set into harder lines. The cashier, sensing her rising ire, slowly shrank behind the assistant manager.

She tried to distract herself again with the phone, to breathe and release, as her new therapist kept telling her. Meredith had always been the high-strung one in their marriage and the source of most conflicts, but after the revelation of Azlyn, her anxiety and the constant arguing with Mike reached new heights. A few months ago, they'd started marriage counseling.

For four years, Meredith had pushed, stuffed, and beaten her feelings about Azlyn so far into a narrow crevice of her heart and mind that she could scarcely reach them anymore. Like dropping something between a car seat and console, utterly unreachable no matter how hard she jammed her hand down to grab them.

And her feelings really weren't about Azlyn herself. They were about Mike keeping such an enormous secret from her all those years. In one therapy session, he'd admitted he was worried while they were dating that Meredith wouldn't marry him if he told her. Then after they were married, he worried she'd leave him if he told her. Then, he had to tell her. His explanation had felt insufficient.

In another session, in a pathetic attempt to inflict pain back at him, Meredith said she'd fucked one of his college friends in a drunken one-night stand a few weeks after she and Mike first met. It didn't create the same level of pain, of course, and Mike had taken it more like a light slap than the gut punch she'd hoped to land.

In the beginning, they'd agreed not to tell anyone beyond immediate family members about the existence of Azlyn while they privately worked through the effects on their marriage. It also allowed Mike and Azlyn to get to know each other better without public pressure. But months turned into a year, and then Maya was born, and Meredith's social media career exploded, and no matter how hard she tried to get past the long betrayal of Mike's secret, the rawer her feelings became. Like dragging a piece of sandpaper across her skin.

Then, yesterday's session. Mike had dealt Meredith a final blow. He was ready to widely share the news about Azlyn. They were closer than ever, and Azlyn gave her blessing.

Barely twenty-four hours' notice to prepare herself, but what was Meredith to say? They'd kept Azlyn's existence secret long enough.

So there she stood in her neighborhood Target store, trying to buy Azlyn's birthday present in time to get it mailed to a college dorm room in Connecticut, knowing Mike was going to post a big social media announcement the following morning when, for the first time, he publicly wished his secret daughter a happy birthday alongside a picture of them together.

As Meredith tapped her credit card harder and harder on the lean pad, she suddenly knew the marriage counseling wasn't helping. And that Mike knew it, too, but neither of them had been able to say it aloud, each waiting for the other to blink first. Despite this realization, getting that damn gift set mailed to Azlyn *by her birthday* still felt like life and death.

More employees joined the tension-filled flurry, buzzing around the registers like nervous insects. Another five minutes, gone. Even if the computer systems magically rebooted that very second and the cashier quickly checked out Meredith's items, and she sprinted out of the store and broke every speed limit, she still couldn't have made it to the post office in time.

She Googled other options and found a nearby FedEx to overnight the gift, which would cost more than the gift itself, but she had no choice.

An overhead speaker crackled and squealed, and a woman's voice cut through the agitated din of unhappy customers.

"Attention Target shoppers, we are currently experiencing a company-wide technical issue with our registers and apologize for this disruption. We've been informed this may take some time to resolve, so we're offering customers the option to leave your selected items in a cart or basket against the wall near the checkout lanes with your name and contact number. When our computer systems are restored, we'll issue a public announcement and you can return and pay for your items. We apologize for this inconvenience. Thank you."

And that was it. That was the moment where all her strangled, repressed feelings from the previous years spectacularly exploded in the form of a single, asshole tweet.

Meredith McCombs @mizmeredesigns ✓

SERIOUSLY @Target registers down nearly 30 min and now telling us to leave baskets and carts with our names on them to come back and pay later?! Unacceptable. I shouldn't have to take time out of my busy day to come back. How are you going to make this right with me? #targetdown #targetfail

It took her less than thirty seconds to type and post it. She hadn't even stepped out of the line and set her basket down before the notifications of replies started lighting up her phone screen, as if it were suddenly electrocuted.

She watched it all with a sense of detachment.

@mizmeredesigns Privileged much????????

@mizmeredesigns Wow why are you acting so awful about this? #targetdown

The replies grew uglier, but she kept reading.

what a bitch @mizmeredesigns

@mizmeredesigns just kill urself and spare the rest of us

Meredith thought about the mega influencer who'd compared herself to Harriet Tubman last month, made some remark about something to do with people cleaning her toilets, and had to go into hiding because of death threats.

Finally, Meredith stopped reading. It didn't matter whether or not she got the gift mailed in time. Or if she promoted a stupid nail polish or candle or gourmet coffee. Her possessed fingers had typed out her own death, each character like pulling pins on grenades, one after another.

She calmly touched the settings wheel from the app menu, scrolled to the red "delete" account button, and tapped it. Other accounts followed. Deleted. Over a decade of pictures, musings, comments, promotions, likes, loves, thoughts, and prayers. Gone. It had never been real. Just like her imagined Spirit Baby.

Meredith gently set down her basket and walked out of the store without leaving her name and number on her items. In her car, she lit a cigarette from the secret pack she kept hidden beneath the front seat. The first inhale and exhale always felt glorious.

She drove a few blocks to Walmart, obeying the speed limit, where she would buy trash bags and tampons.

They would be cheaper there anyway.

Bijou

Eric, this is the story I should've told you before we got married. When you asked me why my previous relationship ended.

I should've told you then but didn't because I was a coward. I lied and said something vague, like the relationship just ran its course, we'd grown apart, blah blah blah.

I don't want any secrets between us, though, so I'm telling you the whole story now.

The day Ryan and I broke up started like it had for months: me sitting at the kitchen table in my pajamas, biding my time until he went to work, so that I could start my job. My *real* job.

Ryan, a creature of habit, poured himself a cup of coffee and buttered a muffin, then ate with his silk tie flipped over his shoulder while studying sports scores on his phone. I sat across from him, drinking my black coffee on an empty stomach, already feeling jittery, and worked on the new Wordle for the day, trying not to look impatient for him to leave.

HOUSE, my starter word back then. Though now, as you know, it's TEAMS.

He asked me, *Did you take a look at that Indeed job I emailed you yesterday? The nanny one in St. Charles?*

Not yet. Haven't had time.

Are you going to look at it today?

Yeah, I will, I said.

I didn't want to be a nanny. But I didn't dare say that.

Ryan continued, *I also connected with an old classmate on LinkedIn. He works for the blood bank. I could ask if they have any openings in HR.*

Sure, I said, even though I didn't want to work in HR or at the blood bank either.

But who was I to be picky? A whole year post-graduation, and I was still pulling only part-time hours in retail hell at The Gap. And Ryan had no idea about my side hustle.

He opened his wallet then and flattened out a crumpled receipt on the table. He told me he'd picked up some toothpaste and a few other toiletries. My half was twelve dollars, or something like that, and could I please Venmo him the money?

I'd stared at the scrawl of his hasty math on the bottom of the receipt.

He asked if it was a problem and laid a hand on top of mine to soften the delivery of the question.

No, no, I said. *It's fine.* I smiled for good measure so he would believe I was giving him the "it-really-is-fine" answer and not the other "fine-but-you're-actually-an-asshole" answer. I didn't want to attract additional scrutiny by picking fights with him over money.

You're an amazing woman, he said. He smiled and leaned in for a quick kiss.

I folded the receipt and tucked it under the saltshaker. I never told you this either, but I had agreed to split expenses with him when we'd moved in together after graduation because it was only fair. He'd gotten hired by a financial company before we even graduated and was virtually debt free since his parents paid for his college education, while I, a useless psychology major, still hadn't found a full-time job because of the shit economy, and was buried in student loan debt because my parents were super fucking poor. But, neither my personal debt nor cash-strapped parents were his fault, or responsibility.

I also never told you that Ryan and I had discussed getting married.

Our first conversation about it was one night while sitting on the steps of the Union after a brutal Western Civ final senior year. We agreed to live together first and get our careers started, then get engaged the following year. But after a year came and went, I still hadn't gotten any form of a career started and was far more preoccupied with when he might pop the question. I kept wondering if he'd surprise me with a romantic dinner and rose-petal-covered house after a mind-numbing day of folding jeans. Or maybe he would pay to have the words *Nicole, will you marry me?* emblazoned across the scoreboard at a Cardinals game. The possibilities had been endless with holidays, birthdays, weekend getaways, and dinners at nice restaurants. (And by the way, your simple, intimate proposal on our favorite park bench at sunset was so much better than anything else I'd childishly dreamed up back then.)

But eventually, my fruitless post-graduation career search had forced Ryan to declare, to my private devastation, that an engagement should wait until I at least found a job. For eighteen more months, he continued to pay the bills and tell me how much I owed him. Rent, utilities, phone, groceries. Even the random three-item grocery charges. The only things in the house we didn't split equally were special foods just one of us ate (Hot Pockets for him, Lean Cuisines for me) and my "girly items," as he put it. He refused to pay for my tampons, although he deemed it reasonable to split the cost of my birth control pills. Fine, I kept telling him, even though it was the other "fine" and I felt, every day, like an elephant was sitting on my chest.

But I never said any of these thoughts out loud, never talked with him about how I felt. Instead, I bottled it all up, tightly screwed down the cap, and kept fantasizing about a wedding.

But pressure, I now know, always has a way of releasing.

THE DAY OF OUR BREAKUP, after Ryan left for work, I made my daily trek to our basic spare bedroom-slash-office-slash-storage room and closed the door behind me. From the closet, I retrieved my ring light stashed behind a box of Christmas decorations, plugged it in, and pointed it at the bed.

Then, from the very back of the closet, hidden behind my old prom dresses and seasonal clothes I never wore anymore, I removed a heavy plastic garment bag.

Inside was the gown.

The "Bijou."

A real Amsale from the famed designer's Blue Label. A strapless silk taffeta wedding gown with a ruched bodice, sweetheart neckline, and giant, handmade taffeta and organza flowers adorning the full skirt. She was so special she had her own name, "Bijou," which felt destined because I'd minored in French, and as you know, I'm a Francophile.

I hung the bag on the door, carefully lowered the zipper, and gave Bijou an adoring stroke as my daily greeting. I just loved staring at her.

I'd found her at an upscale bridal consignment shop in downtown St. Louis one afternoon, several months after moving into the townhouse with Ryan. I'd gone inside the shop just for fun to cheer myself up after another disappointing interview for a counseling job at a youth treatment center. (*You really don't have enough experience. We're looking for someone who can hit the ground running.*) As soon as I'd laid eyes on her, I'd known she was *the one* in the way a person knows another is *the one*, or a couple knows a house is *the one*. I had to have her. I'd been dreaming of my future wedding gown since my freshman year of high school, when, out of boredom, I'd perused Pinterest boards during study hall (when I should've been doing geometry homework) and came across a photo of a gown very similar to Bijou. I'd pinned the image and occasionally brought it up on my phone, dreaming of the day when it would be my turn to buy and wear it as I married the man of my dreams. And there she was in the window of the store, when I least expected to meet her, a near-exact replica of the picture. As soon as I put her on, I'd felt beautiful, successful, and far more amazing than I was.

Purchased new, Bijou retailed for $9,000, but the consignment shop was selling her for a bargain $6,000, and like the saleslady had said, they *never* got the Bijou on consignment, and they'd *just* gotten her that morning, and she'd *surely* be sold by the end of the day. So I had walked out of the store with a cumbersome garment bag and six grand on my Mastercard card (my credit limit), despite barely having enough money in my bank account to buy a tank of gas, despite not having a wedding date, or even an engagement ring. But I told myself I would find a full-time job any day and then get engaged. In the meantime, I'd scrape together the payments, and it wouldn't be a big deal, and it need not concern Ryan.

In the spare bedroom, I switched on the ring light, settled back onto the velvety throw pillows crowding the bed, tapped the little black app icon hidden deep inside my phone files, and logged in with my screen name, @BijouTheBride.

My workday had begun. My real job.

A chat message appeared within a minute.

FrankNFeet: Good morning Bijou. flex and point plz

I angled my phone camera at my bare feet, the ring light nicely catching the sheen of my bright red toenails, and snapped two pictures—one pointed, one flexed—and sent them to the chat.

Bijou: Apprécier mon cherie!

FrankNFeet: yesssssssssssssssss I love red

Frank was a long-haul truck driver with a major foot fetish, but otherwise a harmless and dependable regular.

Back and forth we went for seventeen dollars' worth of texts. Four more chats had started in the meantime. Sixty-seven bucks in fifteen minutes. Then a live call, which charged three times as much as texts.

I'd started the account and side hustle for no other reason than desperation. I hope you understand that. Several months after purchasing Bijou and still no job after dozens of applications (and the Mastercard bill and mounting interest not paying itself), I'd responded to an internet "phone and chat actress" pop-up ad. *Work from home! Set your own schedule! Be your own boss! Make up to $75 an hour!* I saw the dollar signs and couldn't help but click out of curiosity. I completed a lengthy telephone audition, brief online training, picked my screen name because it seemed to be the only name on my brain those days, and was answering texts and calls before I lost my nerve.

In three months, I quickly became one of the most popular operators with my breathy French accent, keen listening skills, and never-ending well of improvised erotic tales. All my regulars knew Bijou The Bride's usual hours—early mornings (after Ryan went to work and before I had to be at The Gap) and late at night (while Ryan was asleep, risky, but he was such a heavy sleeper). At one point, Bijou was a top earner for six weeks straight, and I earned more in a week than I did in a month at The Gap.

Thirty minutes and nearly forty bucks later, the live conversation wound down. I probably said something cringey like, *Au revoir, my bad little boy. I will keep something warm in the oven until next time.* I disconnected the call, and without any new phone or chat requests, got on Pinterest and started scrolling wedding accounts, pinning images I loved. Flower arrangements, cute guest book ideas, bridesmaids' dresses, and unique table settings.

When I stumbled upon an image of a veil, I gasped and immediately pinned it. It was exactly what I'd been looking for—elbow-length silk tulle with a pearl-and-crystal encrusted hair comb. It was exquisite and would match Bijou perfectly. It was $750, which I could easily pay off in a week.

Now, I understood that once I had a full-time job and Ryan and I were officially engaged, I'd be forced to explain how I'd paid for such a lavish gown and accessories. I'd considered several feasible lies: An unexpected inheritance from a dead great-aunt. Long-forgotten savings bonds from my grandparents. A winning lottery ticket. If the dress was already paid for, regardless of my job situation, how could he be mad? But, of course, there would be no reason to reveal the existence of the dress and a lie to cover how it was paid for until there was a full-time job. My life, you see, had become a dead-end street.

Just as I'd closed the Pinterest app and opened my LinkedIn account to read more about the HR job Ryan sent me, I got another call for Bijou. I tapped "accept," and the timer started.

Allo!

Hi, Bijou.

Again, I knew the voice. I switched to speaker. *Ah, Bonjour Gregory! Comment ça va?*

Uh, yeah. Listen, I'm kinda low on money right now, so can we keep this one to around forty bucks?

Poor Gregory. A perpetually broke engineering major with a 4.0 GPA and no luck with the ladies. Sometimes, we skipped the dirty talk, and he just asked me for dating advice.

No problem, I said. *Rapidement today.*

So, what are you wearing?

Common question, and I had a stock answer. *Mon dieu... let me see. Black lace pan-tees, tres sex-ee...* It was always the same. The boy never varied his what-are-you-wearing fantasy, number one on the "most requested" list from training. My fingers drifted back to the Pinterest icon, *tap tap tap*, to the pinned photo of the veil.

I switched positions, my feet propped up against the wall, the phone resting on my chest.

At twenty-six minutes and forty dollars, our conversation ended.

God, you're an amazing woman, Gregory panted.

I froze at his words. Goose pimples crawled up my arms and a burning bile lump formed in the back of my throat.

Um, Bijou?

I collected myself, adjusted the phone.

Ah, oui, Gregory! Our time is up, mon cher. Until next time.

I ended the call and shivered, drawing a soft throw blanket around my arms. Ryan had said the same phrase to me just that morning and had whispered it to me long ago on the steps of the Union, the night we first talked about getting married. *You're an amazing woman.*

I discarded the blanket and rose from the bed, drawn, once again, to the open garment bag hanging on the closet door. I gently ran my fingers over the pristine fabric and delicate beadwork, pushing Gregory's words out of my mind. He was nothing to me, I reminded myself. Just minutes. Just money.

I quickly shed my pajamas in a puddle on the floor and slipped into the gown, zipping it with a handy chain hook I'd bought on Amazon. The press of corset boning against my ribs and swish of crinoline and silk taffeta about my legs almost made me lightheaded. I grabbed a silk Christmas poinsettia from the box in the closet and moved to the cracked full-length mirror propped in the corner of the room.

You're an amazing woman.

Only I uncontrollably heard the words in Gregory's voice and flinched, as if someone had raised a fist to me, and I hurled the ugly fake poinsettias at the mirror.

My phone lit up and chimed again with another call. I carefully perched on the edge of the bed—mindful not to wrinkle the delicate fabric of the gown—and tapped the accept button. The voluminous skirt billowed out around me as if I were sitting on a giant organza mushroom, like Alice in Wonderland.

Allo, I said, but my voice came out sounding flat, uninterested.

Uh, is, is this Bee-joo?

Excitement rippled through my stomach. An unfamiliar voice. A new client. A potential regular. First time calls were always long, and if I kept him on for over an hour, I earned an extra twenty-five percent a minute.

Oui, I answered, forcing my voice higher and lighter. *Il est Bijou.*

Oh, great. My name is…John.

I shook my head. So many of them were named "John" the first time, and it usually took two or more calls for them to get comfortable enough to give me their real names.

Trés bon, John. What would you like to do with Bijou today? Something, how do you say…naughty?

The man laughed, a deep, phlegm-y laugh, and coughed hard to clear his throat. *I'm new at this and a little embarrassed.*

Non-sens! Don't be! Give Bijou your fantasy and she will make it come true.

Okay, then. Let's see. I prefer, like, exotic, tropical places, brunettes, big tits. Oh, and I really love massages. My wife never gives them to me.

I also heard this often—men looking for something they couldn't get from their wives, or rather, their wives were too smart and assertive to refuse—and quickly put together a vivid scenario for him in my mind.

D'accord, John. I will give you a trés sensual massage. First, you are lying on a soft blanket on a secluded beach with no one around. You can hear the waves gently washing against the shore and the rustle of palm trees overhead.

Yeah, that sounds really nice, John breathed as I continued with the details of this exotic island paradise and heard a deep crackle in his lungs whenever he inhaled.

I sit down next to you and start with your head, running my fingers through your hair, scratching lightly with my nails, rubbing your temples. I move down to your neck, nibbling at your ears with my teeth, rubbing out those tight, hard muscles with my fingers.

Yes, yesyesyes…

I talked slowly and re-opened the app with the picture of the veil. I would wear it with the blusher, I decided, so that it could be gently lifted away to reveal my face at the end of the church aisle. Very old-fashioned, perfect for the historical look of the Basilica of St. Louis, his family church. (But wasn't our wedding beneath the Arch so charming?)

As I spoke to John, I drew out the syllables, calculating each word for the digital timer running at the corner of my phone screen. I was already up to fifty-two minutes and had just finished the "massage" portion of the conversation. I laid back and stared at the ceiling, the phone lying on my chest again with the speaker pointed at my mouth.

John intermittently murmured and coughed, a strange, audible combination.

I decided my hair would look best in the veil pinned up and curly because Bijou was a romantic dress, and curls were always soft and romantic, though when I married you, I wore it down in long waves, which was better.

I kept talking, my descriptions growing increasingly graphic.

Nicole?

I bolted upright, and the phone slid off my chest.

Ryan stood in the doorway of the bedroom. His hand was poised on the knob, his other holding his sports coat and, I now saw, his forgotten security badge.

What are you doing? Who are you talking to?

I froze, staring at him, unable to speak or move.

John coughed again. *Bijou? Hello?*

Who are you talking to? Ryan repeated.

Beeejooo? John yelled. *I think we got disconnected!*

I shook my head to regain my wits. *Oh, uh, sorry*, I stuttered. *Pardon moi. One second.* I paused the call and timer and tried to inhale a deep breath, but the tight corset of the dress constricted my lungs.

Why are you wearing a wedding dress? Ryan's tone grew sharper. His face registered confusion, anger, disgust, and hurt all at once. But worse, he looked at me as if he'd never seen me before. As if I were a stranger, some intruder he'd surprised in his own home during a robbery.

Who the hell is on the phone? He planted his feet far apart and crossed his arms tightly over his chest. *Are you fucking cheating on me?*

I opened my mouth to answer, and I really was going to answer him. I'd even previously concocted a lie for that very scenario—telemarketing sales from home for some extra cash, and the dress was on loan from a friend, just to try on for fun—but the words of the pre-prepared lie never came, and all I could do was sit there and stare at him.

I realized in that split second I could let Ryan answer his own question. I was a cheater. A cuckolder. A lying whore of a girlfriend. All of which felt better than the truth of what I'd really been doing.

I'm sorry, I whispered. *I'm so sorry.*

Ryan dropped his arms to his sides, the badge slipping from his fingers and bouncing on the carpet. *Well*, he said, tears filling his eyes, *fuck you, too. This is over.* He bent and picked the badge back up. *Thank God I never bought that goddamn ring.* He was visibly shaking as he said it. He turned and left the room, and seconds later, the front door slammed so hard the windowpanes rattled.

I poised my finger over the disconnect button, ready to cut John off and go after Ryan, to try and explain, tell the truth, and maybe salvage what I could. But my finger just hovered. The clock was paused at fifty-four minutes. Seven more minutes and my rate would go up.

I thought of the pinned photo of the veil once more, the beautiful, lovely veil that would go perfectly with my gown so special it had a name. That name. Bijou, a woman who was bold, assertive, and said what she thought.

A strange sense of calm and relief washed over me. As the engine of Ryan's car revved and tires peeled on the driveway, I tapped the button to resume the call. The clock started counting again.

Ah, pardon moi, John, I said, *but I had to take off my bikini top so you can put some oil on me. Do you want to rub some oil on my bare, golden skin?*

Oh, yes, yes, I do, John said. *You're so good at this. Sogoodsogoodsogood...*

I stood and gazed at my reflection in the mirror once more and nodded.

Yes, Bijou was so good. And that's what I need you to understand most, for a brief time, when I needed her most, she made me feel amazing.

Monkey Mountain

The brothers first heard the screaming one morning as they fed calves. The piercing cries echoed from the timber above the dairy farm, a bluff the family had called "Monkey Mountain" since the brothers were little.

"What the hell was that?" Jamie's breath billowed against the flat pink horizon.

"Shh." Eric frowned.

Seconds passed. A cold gust funneled between the white fiberglass calf huts and swirled early spring snow into Jamie's face.

Another screech splintered the air. Several calves scrambled to the back of their huts.

Eric whispered, "It's an animal."

"What animal sounds like that?" Jamie shivered inside his winter coveralls.

Eric tossed an empty calf bottle into the back of the utility wagon. "Bobcat, maybe." He paused. "Or a mountain lion."

"Bullshit!" Jamie threw an armful of hay into a pen and brushed off the front of his denim coat. "You're lying."

"No, I'm not." Eric cuffed his red nose. "We get 'em sometimes. A couple dozen in the last twenty years or so. Look it up if you don't believe me."

Jamie didn't need to. Even though Eric was eighteen, only two years older, he'd always seemed to be some version of a responsible adult. He could've picked on Jamie anytime he'd wanted to, but he never did.

Eric pulled another empty bottle from a pen. "Don't tell Dad."

"Why not?"

Eric mounted the four-wheeler and started the motor. "We can hunt it ourselves!"

Jamie straddled the back of the seat, trying to imagine a mountain lion strolling through Iowa hills and pastures, hunting for its dinner, but couldn't. The idea seemed ridiculous.

THE FOLLOWING DAY AFTER SCHOOL, Eric and Jamie donned their camouflage hunting clothes, loaded slugs in their 12-gauge shotguns, and started for Monkey Mountain in search of the animal. The boys crossed the shallow Fox Creek, trekked up the snow-dusted bluff and deep into the trees. Eric was a good shot, and even their little sister Lacey loved skeet shooting, but Jamie didn't much like hunting and only did it when his father made him, during deer season. He'd never killed anything, but sometimes it had to be done, he was often reminded. They needed meat; rabid animals were dangerous; dying cattle shouldn't be made to suffer. It was part of farm life and eventually he would have to accept it like any other necessary chore.

The boys silently entered the section of timber that had spawned the nickname Monkey Mountain, a copse of non-native catalpa trees that had been there since Grandpa Chuck bought the farm in the early thirties. As children, Grandpa Chuck told the siblings an absurd tale about some circus performer planting the trees to attract monkeys with the catalpa's long, browned banana-looking seed pods that hung from branches all winter. The kids readily believed their grandfather, and the name Monkey Mountain stuck long after they outgrew the story.

Eric stopped and brushed his gloved fingertips over a short, crooked trunk. "I love it up here," he said.

Jamie rested his gun against his shoulder and plucked a pod from a low branch. He crushed it in his gloved palm. Jamie and Eric had camped amid the trees many times on warm summer nights in a little yellow dome tent. He'd always felt safe there, when it was just the two of them in isolation.

"Do you *really* think there's a mountain lion up here? Or was it something else?" Jamie asked.

Eric shrugged. "Maybe." He tilted his head back, staring up into the branches. "I sure wish Grandpa's story had been true."

"Which one?"

"That there were monkeys up here. It was always my favorite story."

"Yeah, that was a good one." Jamie dropped the pod pieces and switched his gun to the other shoulder. His favorite story from Grandpa Chuck had been his claim that once during a dust storm, he'd witnessed a flock of birds flying backwards to keep from getting dirt in their eyes.

"Are we resting or what?" Jamie asked.

Eric exhaled, sounding tired. "Just for a minute."

Eric had been up since four for the early milking. He'd milked the morning shift before school for years, and Jamie and their father milked the evening shift. Soon Jamie would take on the evening shift by himself. The brothers would eventually take over the farm in a partnership, accepting the reins from their father.

Jamie's toes grew cold inside his boots; he stamped his feet to get some blood flowing. He studied his brother's profile in the fading light. Maybe it wasn't fatigue in his face. *Heart-harried*, their mother called it, whenever Eric became pensive and quiet, as he often did.

An ear-splitting scream spooked the brothers, and Eric aimed his gun in the direction of the sound. Jamie fumbled with his own weapon, struggling to get the safety off and the recoil pad comfortably settled against his shoulder. They waited, fingers on triggers, steel barrels side by side, until another scream tore through the trees.

"God damn," Jamie whispered, "that sounds like a woman being strangled."

Eric shifted his weight and leaned forward.

The screaming continued, a demented, painful growl that echoed off the hillsides. A half mile away, maybe less.

"It *is* a mountain lion," Eric finally said, his voice low. "Sounds like a female."

Jamie's muscles strained to hold up his gun, and the end of the barrel wavered. "How do you know for sure?"

"Me and Corey watched a bunch of big cat YouTube videos in study hall today."

Jamie widened his stance for better balance on the uneven terrain.

"Stop moving," Eric said.

Several minutes passed before another screech echoed, farther away this time.

Eric lowered his barrel. "She's heading east."

Over the next hill, he found fresh scat and a catalpa with claw marks on the trunk. But there, he lost the trail, so the brothers hunkered down in the fallen needles and waited.

Jamie wished he'd thought to bring a couple of warming packs to stick in his coat pockets. He clenched his jaw to try to mask the chatter of his teeth.

Eric burrowed deep into his coveralls until only his eyes were visible over the collar. Last night, after chores, he'd finally had the discussion with his parents he'd been putting off for weeks. The tension at breakfast had been like a taut wire strung across the room that could've been plucked.

The sun began to slide below the horizon, basking the fallow fields and barns in a soft orange light.

"The farm looks so small from up here," Eric said.

"Yeah," Jamie said. "But I like that you can see it all from one place." He picked up a stick and scratched it on the hard ground. "What's going on between you and Mom and Dad?"

The timber was quiet but for the occasional rustle of the wind gently rocking the catalpa pods hanging above their heads.

After a pause, Eric said, "I had to break some news to them."

"What news? You get someone pregnant or something?"

"I told them I applied for college and got in," Eric said. "Engineering at Iowa State. With a scholarship. I leave in August."

Jamie dropped the stick. He lifted his face to the sky and watched the brown pods sway back and forth.

College.

Four years.

Two-and-a-half hours away.

Jamie's throat tightened and he turned away to hide the hot tears welling in his eyes.

"Did you hear what I said?" Eric asked, but Jamie didn't answer. He kept his gaze high in the canopy, blinking tears away.

"I don't want to stay here and farm," Eric said. He kicked at the snow with his boot. "It's hard to explain. Mom and Dad are disappointed."

Jamie didn't know how to respond. He picked the stick back up and chipped at the ground.

A screech echoed from the next hill, and the boys scrambled to their feet. It was close.

Eric lifted his gun to his shoulder and silently motioned to the top of the bluff. He tapped Jamie's chest and pointed right, then tapped his own and pointed left. Jamie nodded, and the boys split up.

Jamie made his way up the western side of the steep hill, taking slow, silent steps. His quads began to burn.

Tiny snowflakes drifted through the trees, dotting his face. Another screech, this one even closer. His heart hammered in his chest. He stopped and fumbled with the rifle to double-check that he'd taken off the safety, which, of course, he already had.

He hadn't fired it in months, since the last time Eric took him target practicing. Had he cleaned and oiled it after the last time? He couldn't remember. Maybe he did oil it. But maybe he oiled it too much and the gun would jam if he tried to fire it. Maybe he would shoot more accurately with his gloves off. He bit the tips and pulled his hands free, leaving the gloves where they landed on the ground.

Just as he repositioned the stock against his shoulder, his peripheral vision caught a sliver of movement. Jamie turned his head toward the bluff, and there she was. Ten, maybe twelve feet above him. She stared back, perfectly still, poised with one front leg bent. She was beautiful with a light cinnamon-colored coat, dark-tipped ears, and black-lined eyes. So much bigger than he'd imagined.

Monkey Mountain was quiet. Jamie and the lion remained locked in a staring contest, like he and Eric used to play when they were kids.

Jamie pressed his cheek against the cold stock and squeezed his left eye shut, sighting with his right. His index finger curled around the trigger.

Shoot it! Jamie's mind screamed at him. *Just shoot it!*

The lion lowered her paw to the ground and took a few steps backward. In a single, blurry motion, the lion launched from the top of the bluff straight at him. Jamie cried out and squeezed the trigger, the violent punch of the butt slamming his shoulder. The lion screeched and hit the ground hard, front legs buckling, her face plowing into the fresh snow.

Jamie lowered the gun barrel, his ears ringing. Acrid haze drifted into his face and clogged his nostrils. The lion lay just a few feet in front of him on her side, unmoving. He waited until her shallow breaths ceased and took a step toward her.

One red entry wound marked the left side of her neck, her eyes glassy and fixed.

He kneeled next to her and laid his bare hand on her warm belly, stroking her coarse hair.

Footsteps pounded down the hill above him.

"Jamie!" Eric shouted, panting. "Jamie!"

Eric halted, mouth agape, when he saw Jamie and the prone animal. He crouched next to Jamie and laid his shotgun down on the ground.

"I got her," Jamie said quietly.

The snow fell thicker now, covering everything in a smooth white blanket. Jamie lifted his face to the sky and let the cold flakes gather on his eyelashes.

"Great shot," Eric said.

Jamie gave him a small smile.

"Sometimes it has to be done," he said.

Confess and Guess

From: wuthrich.eric@TerisChem.com
Sent: Wednesday, January 12 10:25am
To: nmwuthrich@STLBehavioralHealth.org
Subject: Something To Tell You

Dear Nicole,

Ever since game night at the Dohertys' house last weekend, I've been wanting to tell you something, and finally decided to just put it in an email. You were brave enough to tell me the truth about what really happened with your ex and your wedding dress, so it only feels fair to tell you about this story from my college days.

When we were all playing Confess and Guess, the one "yes" answer to the card *Have you ever left someone on the side of the road?* was mine, not Tyler's like everyone thought.

This is the story of what happened.

My sophomore year of college, I had a dumpy off-campus apartment on the far west side of the city and rode the uni bus every Monday and Wednesday morning for an 8 a.m. Calculus class I hated and was flunking.

The route, the Red Line, always had the same driver: Chester.

There were just two passengers at the beginning of the route: me and an old woman with a walker whose name I didn't know.

One freezing February morning, Chester picked up me and then the old woman at her usual stop, Clemens Boulevard, and lowered the liftgate for her to get on board. *Walker-shuffle-shuffle-walker.*

She sat in the front while I sat in the middle. It was midterms week, and I needed at least a "C" on the Calc test if I had any hope of passing the class. I'd stayed up until four in the morning studying, slept a couple of hours, pounded two Red Bulls, reviewed my notes again, and left, anxious as shit.

Two blocks later, though, the bus suddenly lurched to a hard stop. Without a word, Chester leapt out of his seat, shoved open the double doors, and ran—no, absolutely fucking *sprinted*—down the middle of the street.

I remember standing up, confused, watching Chester's large form grow smaller until he turned a corner, bulky arms still pumping hard and huge plumes of breath blooming above his head, and disappeared.

What the fuck? I said.

My confusion was quickly replaced with modern day panic, I ducked to the dirty floor and covered my head, fearing it was a shooting. It's our entire generation's default mode, right? Duck and cover.

I waited for several seconds in my fetal position, but there was nothing. No sounds, no expected *pop pop pops,* or people screaming. The residential neighborhood was silent, except for the humming motor of the bus.

I uncurled my body and slowly rose, still cowering behind the seats.

It was just me and the old woman, and when she looked at me, I could see she was frightened.

I asked if we should wait, but she just shrugged.

The whole thing was so weird. I didn't know what the hell to make of any of it. Get off the bus? Run? Stay and wait?

I walked to the front and stupidly stared at the crowded control panel. The two-way radio was silent. I lifted the mic and pressed the button on the side as I spoke.

Hello? Hello? Hello? Anyone? Can you help? I'm a passenger and our driver just left us here.

Me and the old lady stared at each other while we waited for a response.

Silence. No reply.

The bus motor briefly shuddered, but kept running. I replaced the mic and looked around the neighborhood again. It was disturbingly empty. Not a single car, person, or animal anywhere in sight. Not even a passing car.

What the fuck, I said again, even craning my neck to look up at the sky. Nothing but a few puffy white clouds.

I slumped into the driver's seat and drummed my fingers on the wheel. Checked the time on my phone. Thirteen minutes until eight.

Fuck. I couldn't be late for that Calc test. The proctor always locked the door at precisely 8 a.m. sharp, no exceptions.

I Googled the city transportation department for a phone number, but when I called, it just took me in auto-response circles.

I disconnected.

We were still several blocks from campus, too far to make it on foot. I could probably catch the Green Line if I ran to the next stop.

I think we should get off, I said to the old woman.

Okay, she answered, her voice shaky. *But I have to use the lift. I can't get down the stairs.*

I looked back at her, gripping the sides of her walker, then at the mechanical lift, then at the dizzying control panel again.

I dropped my face into my hands.

I could not miss that test.

Finally, a car approached from behind the bus, and slowly pulled around, the outline of the single passenger barely visible through the heavily tinted windows. The car stopped at the bus driver's window and just idled, the motor loudly revving. I stared into the black hole of the windows, into nothing, as dread crept up the back of my neck.

The car tires suddenly peeled out and it sped away.

I stood and threw my hands in the air and shouted, *What the fuuuuck!*

I paced up and down the aisle, fighting the rising panic in my chest.

If I didn't pass that midterm, I'd lose my private scholarship. And without the scholarship, I couldn't afford to stay in school. And I couldn't go back home as a failure. Especially after hurting my family so much by leaving in the first place.

So, on that cold ass day in February, standing on that stupid bus after Chester bolted, after the car did the creepy slow drive by, and with all that heavy shit running through my mind and about to miss my midterm, I did the most shameful thing I've ever done.

I grabbed my backpack from my seat, hurried past the old lady and her walker, jumped off the bus, and started running for the next stop. I pumped my arms and legs as hard as I could, my backpack slamming into my shoulders with my cheap used laptop inside. And I started to cry. Tears and snot poured down my face and I was huffing so hard I thought my chest would explode, but I kept fucking running, and never once looked back at that bus with the old lady still inside.

I made it to the next stop just as the Green Line was closing its doors and pulling away. I screamed at the driver, and she took pity on me. Stopped and let me on. Saw my face, beet red and tears and snot, and told me to take a deep breath. I'd made it.

I collapsed into a seat and dropped my head between my knees, trying not to puke. And not just from running. I didn't tell the next Green Line driver what happened on the Red Line. I couldn't speak.

When I exited at the next stop, I ran across campus to Carver Hall, where I got to the testing room just as the proctor was reaching for the doorknob to close the door. He saw me coming and hurried to shut it like the asshole he always was, but I barely squeaked through the opening, catching the sleeve of my nylon coat on the latch and making a small tear in the fabric that I would wear for the remaining years of school. Sometimes, girls would see the tear and poke a thin, delicate finger into it and say, *Hey, you have a hole in your coat*. And I'd dumbly look at it and reply, *Oh, really? I hadn't noticed.*

After I dropped into a seat, the proctor looked at me and said, *I was feeling nice today and let you in.*

I wanted to fucking deck him.

I pulled off my stupid *I♥Hot Moms* knit stocking cap I loved so much that year (a Christmas gift from Jamie), tucked it into my bag, and logged onto a computer to take the test. My hands shook the entire time, and I could barely concentrate.

And here's the thing. I flunked the test.

I had to retake Calc that summer to stay eligible for my scholarship. I passed with a B+.

Two days after bombing that midterm, I boarded the Red Line again, another freezing February morning, for my Wednesday class. There was a new driver, a woman, who said nothing. Not a single word about what had happened on Monday, or what became of Chester.

At the next stop, the old woman was sitting on the bench, as usual, and walked to the bus lift. *Walker-shuffle-shuffle-walker.*

As the new driver lowered the electric lift, I slunk down in my seat, dropped my head, and closed my eyes, pretending I was asleep.

She sat in her usual seat, and the bus moved on.

More passengers got on and off, but I kept my eyes closed, fake sleeping.

At the first stop downtown, which I knew was the old lady's exit, I opened my eyes to peek at her.

She hoisted herself to her feet using her walker, slid the strap of her purse over her shoulder, and turned around. She looked directly at me and flipped me the bird.

She then moved up the aisle, exited on the lift. *Walker-shuffle-shuffle-walker* down the sidewalk.

I never saw her again.

The next week, I started getting up ten minutes earlier to walk an extra three blocks to a different bus stop.

I never knew the lady's name, where she lived, where she was going all those mornings, or how she finally got off the stranded Red Line.

And I never learned what the fuck happened to Chester.

There was no big life lesson in that moment and the shame it caused me.

But here's the thing, Nic. Because I had to stay on campus that summer to retake Calc, my longtime girlfriend back home met someone else and broke up with me. And because I was so damn broke and bored, I got a second job at Lowe's where I met Tyler, and we became great friends, and both got jobs in St. Louis, where he met Louisa, who was friends with you, and introduced us a few months after your previous relationship ended.

If the thing with your wedding dress and the uni bus incident did not happen, we might never have met. Turns out, our confessions brought us together.

Who would've guessed.

Love,

e

The Girl in the Pipe

I remembered breathing dirt.

Gritty, black Iowa dirt that made me cough and choke.

I remembered darkness and constriction, and I remembered voices echoing from above. My older sister, shouting, "Are you down there, Martha J*ooooo*?"

Two days before my fourth birthday, I fell nineteen feet down a pipe, becoming lodged before I reached the bottom.

It remained a great mystery how I got there in the first place. Even I didn't know how I got there because I remembered very little. Bits and pieces, really.

The pipe was actually an abandoned dry well in my uncle's old hay barn he sometimes used for beef cattle. The pipe head stuck barely two feet above ground and ran twenty-seven feet deep. The circumference was a mere nine-and-a-half inches. I fell feet first and became lodged at the nineteen-foot mark, suspended with my left leg dangling, my right bent at the knee and pinned to my chest, and my arms stuck above my head. I was rescued thirty-one hours later, on my fourth birthday.

On the ten-year anniversary of my rescue, my family gathered at my uncle's farm, inside the paddock of the weathered old barn with the now-sealed metal pipe head. My mother and Aunt Kathy decorated the paddock with multi-colored streamers and balloons that shriveled in the heat before the party even started. My sixteen-year-old sister Kelly sat in a lawn chair in the corner with her sketchbook, talking to no one.

Two days before the party, I started thinking about statistics and percentages and probability. The percentage of four-year-old children who could fit through a nine-and-a-half-inch circle. The probability of how I ended up in that position. Statistically, how many children could even survive the initial fall, and how many wouldn't.

When Kelly and I were children, Uncle D babysat us on weekends while my mother and Aunt Kathy cleaned houses in town. He would catch garter snakes and chase us around the yard yelling, *Give it a kiss!* as we screamed and ran away. He was the grown-up who discovered I was in the pipe. Kelly and I had been playing in the barn, and when Uncle D entered the paddock to get us for lunch, he found my sister standing calmly next to the pipe head, and the large rock normally covering the opening resting on the ground. Kelly was eerily alone, he said, and he was confused. But then he heard the terrible echo of a crying child. When he asked, "Where's Martha Jo?" Kelly silently pointed at the pipe. The rest, he used to say, is history.

Only one local newspaper reporter came to the anniversary party, but at the time of my fall into the pipe, there were dozens of reporters and news crews from all over the country, parked up and down the road in front of the farm. My rescue was a big deal.

After the party started, the woman who drove my school bus years ago waved at me. "Martha Jo, come get a picture with me!" she said.

I couldn't remember her name, so I just smiled and posed next to her with the pipe head between us. After my rescue, it was filled with gravel and capped with a metal lid. The rescue tunnels were also filled long ago. One twenty-foot vertical shaft, and one two-foot horizontal tunnel. I vaguely remember the vibrations of jackhammers when the tunnels were being dug.

More party guests arrived, and the barn quickly grew hot. I started to sweat through my *Martha Jo Watkins, America's Little Girl!* T-shirt with puffy pink fabric paint my mother made me wear.

After the picture with my former bus driver—whose name I couldn't remember because we only lived on that route for one year—two brothers who I also rode on the bus with asked me to stand with them next to the pipe for a picture. Then their younger sister, who had been Kelly's seatmate. I couldn't remember the sister's name, but remembered the brothers. They looked so much older now, practically men. I felt childish in my puffy paint shirt.

I was used to requests for pictures, or for my autograph. Someone would hear or read my name, *Martha Jo Watkins,* and recognition would flicker across their face. I could almost see them searching the deepest corners of their memories for the name before they inevitably gasped and snapped their fingers. "You're that little girl in the pipe!"

Yes, that was me.

I stood for the pictures. I signed whatever it was they want me to sign. I've always had nice cursive.

Martha Jo Watkins

But I was always a disappointment to people when they recognized me and asked for details I couldn't provide. *Traumatic Amnesia,* a doctor once called it.

That's why I'd decided I no longer wanted to be called Martha Jo once I started high school in the fall. I wanted instead to be called Marty. It sounded edgier. Cooler. Marty was a girl who got invited to parties and cut classes to vape behind the football field. Martha Jo wasn't cool. Martha Jo didn't get invited to parties or cut classes. Martha Jo was the little freak who fell into the well.

I figured no one would recognize the name Marty Watkins. Marty Watkins wasn't the little girl in the pipe. Marty Watkins wouldn't get pestered with questions from nurses, dental hygienists, or teachers about what happened, what I remembered, or what it was like to go on *The Today Show* and talk about *how on earth you got into that tiny pipe!* And even though Marty Watkins would always have a limp because she had two gangrenous toes amputated, and she'd still have a massive scar on her knee from skin graft surgeries, she at least wouldn't be so easily recognized by her name.

My mother frantically waved to me from the other side of the barn. "Martha, come here!"

I crossed the powdery dirt floor, my rubber flip flops flicking up dust behind me, and joined my mother and an older man.

"Martha," my mother said breathlessly, still ignoring my name change request, "this is Bob Rushing, the man who pulled you from the pipe. Do you remember him?"

Of course I didn't remember him. I only recognized him from photos I'd seen on the internet. He was a fireman from another county who showed up at Uncle D's barn after my story broke on the evening news. Bob Rushing, the hero of the day because he was born without collar bones and could freakishly collapse his shoulders, making him the only adult who could fit through the narrow rescue tunnels to pull me out.

"You're all grown up," Bob said. His eyes became watery. He hugged me and I half-heartedly hugged him back. I could tell Bob was a kind man and that I meant a great deal to him, and even though I was grateful for what he did, he was still a stranger to me. His memories and my memories of that August day were very different.

Bob released me and patted the top of my head. "You were so tiny back then! Like a little doll! But you were such a trooper."

I had heard that before, too; I'd been small my entire life, and was especially small for a four-year-old. No one dreamed a child could fit into that pipe opening, but lo and behold, I did.

"We talked to you constantly," Bob continued, "and you sang to us."

"'I See the Moon,'" my mother interjected, also teary now. "I sang it to her as a baby." She took a breath and started. "*I see the moon and the moon sees me. The moon sees the one that I long to see.*"

Bob joined her. His voice was deep and kind of nice. "*So, God bless the moon and God bless me. And God bless the one that I long to see.*"

I stood dumbly in front of them, embarrassed. They were singing and it was weird.

They wiped their eyes and hugged each other. The lone reporter from the local paper approached. She'd been listening and wanted to talk to Bob. I was relieved and slipped away, unnoticed.

I didn't remember the singing, or talking to the people above. For so long, I only remembered breathing dirt, and feeling vibrations.

Until this week, when I started to remember other things. Frozen images, flashes of sounds. My sister's echoing voice, calling my name. *Martha Jooooo?*

I remembered a coloring book of ladybugs from Uncle D. A plastic bucket overflowing with Crayolas, some snapped in half with dull tips and paper wrappers peeling off like a snake shedding skin.

Earlier that morning, as I watched my mother and Aunt Kathy decorate the barn paddock, I remembered my sister burying the two of us beneath a pile of scratchy hay in the loft.

Don't make a sound, she'd whispered. *He won't find us here.*

Or did she say, *You'll be safe down there*? I remembered both, and the wires kept crossing.

After escaping my mother and Bob Rushing, my sister pinched the back of my arm, and I startled.

"Dad's here," she said.

I turned and looked around. "Where?"

Kelly nodded over her shoulder, and I spotted him crossing the yard. We hadn't seen him in months. He entered the paddock and stopped, appearing uncomfortable, like he didn't belong. I'd never lived with our father. He moved out and divorced my mother while she was still pregnant with me. He was there for the whole pipe ordeal, though. I'd watched videos of him on YouTube, being interviewed, crying, asking for prayers even though he'd never gone to church that I knew of. Kelly said it was the most time he'd ever spent with either of us.

We made eye contact, he approached, and we hugged. We chatted about the decorations and newspaper reporter and quickly ran out of things to say. He felt like Bob Rushing to me. A stranger.

He also hugged Kelly, but she didn't hug him back. He turned away and started talking to someone else, and that was the end of our interactions for the day.

Kelly grabbed a handful of peanuts from a bowl on the refreshments table. "I don't know why he bothered coming," she said. "He was never around when we actually needed him."

I took a peanut from her palm and tossed it into my mouth, shrugging. I'd never given him much thought.

"Come on," she said. "Let's get the hell out of here." She tugged on the sleeve of my stupid puff paint shirt, and I followed her into the adjacent corral. We climbed a wooden ladder into the hay loft, which was still full of brown and brittle hay.

I'd loved the barn since I was a kid, especially the loft. Kelly and I spent hours up there, playing house, playing school, trying to save and hatch baby bird eggs that had fallen out of nests from the rafters. We'd scribbled our names on the wooden wall boards in pencil, and built a wobbly table out of pieces of a broken crate and rusty nails we found in an old coffee can.

Kelly flopped backwards onto the hay pile and closed her eyes. I sat next to her, drawing my knees to my chest. I thought again about the image of her burying me beneath the hay, the day I fell down the pipe. I heard her voice as she laid armfuls over me, making me sneeze.

Don't make a sound. He won't find us here.

I remembered her whispering.

You'll be safe down there.

That's what she said. I was sure of it.

Suddenly, I remembered scrapes on my palms. My arms growing tired.

You'll be safe down there.

I was hanging.

Kelly stirred in the hay next to me. I laid back and stared at the rafters full of crumbling sparrow nests.

"What do you remember about that day?" I asked. "When I fell into the pipe?"

She didn't answer. A barn swallow fluttered from one rafter to another.

"I remember bits and pieces," I finally said. "But lately, I've been remembering more."

Kelly turned her head to look at me.

"You buried us beneath the hay," I continued. "You'd done it before."

She reached out and took my hand. Squeezed it hard.

"We were hiding, weren't we?" I said quietly. My stomach felt slimy saying it out loud.

Someone in the paddock laughed loudly.

"The pipe," I said, "I was holding onto the edge." As I uttered the words, I knew I'd had the memory all along, buried somewhere deep in my brain, waiting for me to finally discover it.

Kelly released my hand and rolled over, away from me.

"You lowered me inside," I whispered. "You said I would be safe down there."

She didn't answer.

Another barn swallow fluttered around the rafters, startled by more laughter below.

I hugged my knees again and pressed my forehead to them, Kelly's little six-year-old voice echoing around my skull. *You'll be safe . . . You'll be safe . . . You'll be safe . . .*

Her little voice, the words suddenly sharpened in my memory. My head snapped up.

"From him," I said.

Kelly sat upright and stared at me. Her cheek was red from where she'd laid against the scratchy hay. "What?"

I looked at her. "You said, 'You'll be safe down there *from him*.' Didn't you? From Uncle D?"

The tip of Kelly's nose turned red as her eyes brimmed with tears. "I thought you would be strong enough to hold on," she spoke at last.

At that moment, I felt like I wanted to cry, too. I touched her shoulder. I didn't know what to say.

"Girls?" Aunt Kathy shouted from the bottom of the ladder. "Are you up there?"

Kelly abruptly stood and brushed hay from her clothes. "But at least he never got to you." She smiled weakly at me, and scrambled down the ladder.

"There you are!" I heard Aunt Kathy say below. "Your mother is looking for you. Where's Martha Jo?"

"She's coming," Kelly answered.

I couldn't move from the dusty hay pile. I kept staring at the barn swallows, unable to blink. I thought my eyeballs would dry out and shrivel up like grapes.

I wondered if *traumatic paralysis* was a thing. Like my traumatic amnesia. Maybe I had both.

But finally, I blinked. I sat up. I was fine.

I was safe. Because of my sister.

I climbed down the ladder where Aunt Kathy was waiting to scold me for disappearing during my own party. Beads of sweat dotted her upper lip, and I could tell she'd waxed it that morning because the skin was red and irritated.

"You and your sister," she huffed. "Always disappearing, ever since you were kids."

I glanced at Kelly, and she gave me a look, an expression I understood without having to be told. I said nothing.

My mother approached. She was so happy. So was my dad, still yapping away with a neighbor I didn't know, and Aunt Kathy, and Bob Rushing, and the bus driver. They all seemed so happy.

Except Kelly, who sat back down into her camping chair and quietly picked up her sketch book once more.

"The newspaper wants a picture of you in front of the pipe," my mother said. She plucked a piece of hay out of my hair.

I obeyed, as I always did, and stood stiffly in front of the pipe head. I forced a smile for the reporter, because I knew who everyone needed me to be: Martha Jo Watkins, America's Little Girl.

The girl in the pipe.

That Time I Didn't Tell a Grownup

When I was in sixth grade, a new girl started riding my bus. Her name was Kelly, and we became seatmates, assigned by our bus driver, to the seat over the wheel hump. Kelly always sat next to the window; I sat by the aisle. We had a long route in our part of the county, a typical southern Iowa swath punctuated by narrow gravel roads, trailers with rusted siding, and snarling, skinny dogs chained up in every other yard.

Kelly was thirteen and a year older than me, and had just moved to a little house on our route, with her mother and younger sister. Her sister walked with a limp because she once fell down some hole when she was a toddler, and apparently her rescue was all over the news. I never talked to her, but I did talk to Kelly during our rides to and from school. We weren't really friends, but we chatted about teachers and kids in our classes, and sometimes she helped me with my math homework because I was terrible at story problems.

The first day I met Kelly on the bus, I immediately noticed she was carrying a small red vinyl purse instead of a back-pack, wore glittery blue shadow the same shade as her eyes, and heavy foundation that created a boundary line along her jawline, like a map delineating states. My mother was strict and wouldn't allow me to wear make-up until I turned thirteen, so I still looked like a freckle-faced little kid at the start of sixth grade.

It would be fair to say I was jealous of Kelly, but what I envied most about her wasn't the purse or make-up, but that she wore a bra. Not a training bra or sports bra—but a *real* bra, because she actually needed one. I'd started wearing a tiny white cotton trainer over the summer even though I didn't need one, and it constantly rode up the front of my flat chest, creating lumpy ripples beneath my shirts. But, I stubbornly wore it anyway because no one wants to be the last person in anything.

On Friday afternoons, Kelly and her sister would get dropped off at their aunt and uncle's farmhouse, which was just down the road from her house. Aunt Kathy and Uncle D, she called him. Kelly said they stayed there on the weekends while her mother worked, and that she couldn't wait to turn thirteen so she could watch her sister, and they wouldn't have to go to the farm anymore.

One morning during our bus ride, I started talking with the boy who sat in the seat across from us. His name was Brady, and he was also in seventh grade. I'd had a crush on him since the beginning of the school year. He'd grown taller and had gotten his braces removed over the summer, and just like that I was in love with him, doodling his name all over the pages of my notebooks, even though he completely ignored me. I'd been patiently waiting for an opportunity to talk to him and finally struck up a conversation by asking about a splint on his wrist. He told me he'd sprained it from a wreck on his dirt bike over the weekend.

Out of nowhere, Brady then said to me, "You're really flat-chested for a sixth grader. Boys don't like flat chested girls." Then promptly went back to ignoring me.

I turned away, tears of humiliation stinging my eyes.

Kelly, who had been drawing a cartoon picture of a horse in a sketch pad, saw my tears, my quivering chin, and asked. "What's the matter?"

I quietly confided in her about my crush on Brady, and what he'd just said.

Kelly gave me a tissue from a small package she kept in the red purse. "All girls' bodies develop in their own time," she said. "Your time will come when you'll need a real bra, you'll see. And anyways, boys are fucking idiots."

I laughed and dried my tears, feeling better. She patted my knee and gave me the cartoon drawing of the horse.

A few stops later, Kelly turned to me and said, "Can I tell you something, too?"

I nodded.

"Sometimes my Uncle D kisses me and stuff. I take off my clothes and he does things to me."

I think that's what she said. Something along those lines. I don't remember her exact words, but I distinctly remember the expression on her face.

Matter of fact.

As if she'd told me the sky was blue.

I didn't know what to say. Seconds passed in silence. An uncomfortable knot tightened in the pit of my stomach, and my face flushed.

Kelly stared at me, waiting for a response. Any response. But, I didn't have one.

Instead, I laughed. A tight, nervous laugh.

I don't know why I laughed. Maybe it was discomfort, or that I wanted to pass it off like she was joking to make myself feel less uncomfortable, or maybe I was just a stupid kid. An idiot. Like the boys she'd mentioned.

It doesn't matter. Because after I laughed at her, her mouth turned down at the corners, and she sighed quietly and looked away. She didn't speak to me for the rest of the ride to school, or during the ride home. She just stared out the window, her hand clasped tightly, resting on her little red vinyl purse and sketch pad in her lap.

That evening during dinner, I sat at my family's long kitchen table as my older brothers talked noisily over each other with food in their mouths, and couldn't stop thinking about what Kelly had told me.

My mother, sitting next to me, said, "You seem heart-harried tonight. What's the matter?"

I rolled a shriveled pea around my plate with my fork.

"Nothing," I answered. "I'm tired. I don't feel well."

She felt my forehead, cupped my cheeks between her soft hands. "No fever," she said. "Go to bed. You're probably coming down with something."

I stood and left the table without telling her.

I could've told my mother. She would've done something, I'm sure of it. Called Kelly's mother or aunt. Called the school. Called the bus driver, a nice lady who gave us candy canes at Christmas. My mother was no nonsense like that. But I didn't tell her. I said nothing.

That night, unable to sleep, I got up, tiptoed across the hall, and knocked lightly on the door of my brothers' shared room. Eric was still doing homework at the desk in the corner. A small lamp illuminated his pencil dancing across a sheet of paper. Jamie slept soundly in his twin bed, his feet nearly hanging off the end.

"Eric," I whispered. "I can't sleep."

"Why? What's wrong?"

I was close to Eric. He was brave and always did the right thing, no matter what. I tried to form the words, to tell him what Kelly had said to me on the bus that day.

"Nothing," I finally answered. "Just thought I heard something."

I went back to my room.

I could've told Eric. He would've done something, I'm sure of it. Told our mother. Told the bus driver. Maybe even told off Kelly's Uncle D.

The next morning, I mounted the steps of the bus and took my seat next to Kelly.

She looked as she always did: blue eyeshadow, foundation like a coat of paint, carrying the red purse. She bent intently over her sketch pad drawing a new picture. A cartoon dog with funny ears and big eyes.

At the next stop, Kelly closed the sketch book, produced a stick of spearmint gum from her backpack, leaned over my knees, and held it out across the aisle to Brady.

"Gum?" she said and smiled.

He smiled back. Accepted the foil-wrapped stick. "Thanks."

She didn't offer a piece to me.

"What kind of dirt bike do you ride?" she asked Brady.

"Yamaha," he answered.

"I love Yamahas," she said.

And they started talking about engines and chains and sprockets.

They talked the next day, too, and the day after that.

Since she always sat next to the window, Kelly would lean forward and talk around me, as if I were a shrub. Sometimes, she wore blouses that would gape open when she leaned over, exposing her cleavage and flashes of her real bras, which were pink and pale blue with lacy edges.

Brady would stare when this happened, his eyeballs drawn to the peeking bras like the ends of two magnets.

"Do you want to see something?" Kelly asked him after several days of these flirty conversations.

"Sure," he said.

I opened my social studies book and pretended to read, trying to ignore them both.

Kelly straightened and checked over the tops of the seats that no one was watching, then hunched back down. In my periphery, I saw her unbutton the top buttons of her blouse, pull her lacy blue bra to the side, and expose her right breast and round, pink nipple.

My cheeks caught fire. I noisily flipped a page.

Brady laughed and half-heartedly hid his face behind his hands, pretending to be shocked, though he lowered them after a few seconds.

"You know what my dad says?" he asked her.

"What?"

"That girls' tits are the only thing you can look down on and approve of at the same time."

Kelly fake-laughed and covered herself. "That's funny."

I fake-read my book and said nothing.

I thought about another joke Brady had once told me, before he declared my tits were too small to look down on, a rhyme with finger gestures to go along with it that I, too, had laughed at.

Good girls sit like this. His index and middle fingers pressed firmly together. *Bad girls sit like that.* Middle finger crossed over index finger. *But girls who sit like this,* index and middle finger splayed wide, *get this,* middle finger stuck straight in the air, *like that,* finger snap.

After Kelly secured the last button, I looked at her. *That's right,* I thought angrily, *that's what girls like you get.*

The next day, Kelly unbuttoned her shirt again and exposed her breast, and again the day after that. Sometimes she showed only one, sometimes she showed both.

And Brady continued to laugh and cover his face, but after a while, he didn't even bother covering his eyes anymore.

The school year and peep show bus rides dragged on. Kelly never spoke to me again.

The following school year, I got on the bus as a seventh grader, but Kelly wasn't there. She had moved with her mother and little sister with the limp over the summer, a classmate later told me. No one knew why or where they'd moved this time.

I sat by myself. I did my own story problems.

After a few days, Brady leaned across the aisle and asked me if I knew where Kelly had gone.

"Who cares," I said.

"You're in a bitchy mood," he said, and laughed. "What's the matter? PMS?"

I stared at him. "You're a fucking idiot," I said, and satisfyingly saw the power of my razored words slice him.

Brady scooted back into his seat and clamped his arms over his chest, scowling. He never tried to talk to me again, but I didn't care.

I no longer had crushes on boys like Brady. And over the summer I'd started wearing eyeshadow and finally needed a real bra, just like Kelly said I would.

Release of Information

A young man's face appeared on the computer screen, or what was left of his face. His forehead and hairline were a bloody, shredded mess. His left eyebrow had been completely sheared off. Broken nose. Broken teeth. The summary report:

42-year-old male transported to ED by ambulance…left pneumothorax…left rib fracture… fractured clavicle… left distal radius fracture…severe facial lacerations… acute alcohol intoxication….301 BAC.

A driver so drunk he should have been dead from alcohol poisoning.

In the Des Moines County Hospital medical records department, Kara Morton spent her days doing exactly what her job title described: releasing information from hospital medical records.

Not so long ago, when she was still using, it could've been Kara with broken bones and half her face stitched up like Frankenstein. She'd once nodded off and fallen head-first into a sliding glass door but somehow ended up with only a small cut above her eye. Whenever she came across the records of addicts, she always looked at the photos. They were more sobering than attending a meeting.

Kara opened an email for another request. A lab report request from an endocrinologist. Quick and easy.

Her cell phone vibrated. A text message from Paul appeared. *How does spaghetti sound?*

Yum! She texted back. *Should I pick up breadsticks?*

No need. Making from scratch. Just for you Xoxo

Kara smiled. *Xoxo*

Paul was Kara's fiancé. They'd met two years ago when she'd gone to a Grace Church of Christ coat drive one brittle November Saturday looking for a free hand-me-down after a junkie boyfriend burned all her clothes in the backyard during a fight. There, in the warm and unthreateningly beige-colored Fellowship Hall, while sorting through gently used L.L. Bean and North Face parkas, Paul first spoke to her. "What size do you wear?"

He'd seemingly zeroed in on Kara. She knew what he must have seen—a skinny, stringy-haired heroin addict he just couldn't resist trying to save. He fitted Kara with a decent maroon Eddie Bauer ski jacket, gloves, and a wool cap, quickly introduced her to the Grace AA meetings facilitator. Before she knew it, the church had found her a bed in a nearby rehab center. She was surprised how easily she agreed. Or maybe she'd just been exhausted from the years of using, and was finally ready to quit.

After finishing her ninety days, she got a sponsor, reconciled with her parents and older brother Jay, joined Grace Church, and got the hospital job. Her recovery had been so swift it was downright startling. Everything she had now, she owed to Paul and the church, and she continued to wear the maroon ski jacket as a reminder.

She texted Paul again. *Only 45 more minutes!*

He replied with a thumbs up followed by a red heart.

At five minutes to five, Kara gathered her stack of envelopes to drop in the mail bin on her way out. Val, the office receptionist, approached her desk. "Hey, don't leave yet. I just forwarded you an email," she said. "Records request from a gynecologist in West Des Moines. He wants it before the end of the day."

"Okay." Kara sighed and set the stack of envelopes back down.

"Big plans for tonight?" Val asked.

"Nothing too exciting." Kara opened her email and clicked on the new message. "Just our usual Friday—"

Her gaze snagged on the first line.

Medical Records request for
Des Moines Regional County Hospital
Emergency Room Report
Patient: Rachel R. Graves
ED date: July 21

"Your usual Friday what?" Val said and then laughed. "What's wrong?"

Kara snapped her head up and instantly plastered a smile on her face. "Sorry! I just meant, you know, our usual Friday, that's it. Staying in."

Val slipped on her coat. "Well, have a good weekend."

"You, too."

The second Val left, Kara quickly entered the name and date of the ER visit. As a small circle spun in the center of her slow computer searching the hospital database, Kara anxiously bounced her knee up and down.

Rachel R. Graves.

Paul's Rachel.

Before there was Paul and Kara, there was Paul and Rachel.

Rachel had been another Grace Church member, and her parents used to be close friends with Paul's. During late high school and into college, Paul and Rachel had "courted"—the church's strict rule of supervised, nonsexual dating with the intention of marriage that comprised of chaste side hugs and chaperoned outings to places like Cracker Barrel. For six years, they had been a perfect couple. She was the beautiful star of the church choir; he was the handsome rising outreach leader under the pastor's tutelage. But halfway through their junior year at university, Rachel had abruptly, shockingly, ended the relationship, and left the church with no explanation. Her parents mysteriously resigned from the church not long after. Rachel eventually moved to Minneapolis for some marketing job and started a new life no one ever talked about, as if she'd died. Paul had been heartbroken, so devastated he rarely spoke of it, or even her name.

Kara had pieced the story together from other church members, old rumors resurfacing.

Rachel had an affair. Stole money from Paul's mother. Become promiscuous. Became a lesbian. No one really knew. But the legacy of her former-sterling reputation lingered.

Paul and Rachel, once the golden couple of Grace Church.

On Kara's computer screen, finally, Rachel's name and record number appeared in the patient registry.

GR10028.

Kara clicked on the file.

Admitting complaint: acute abdominal pain and bleeding post elective pregnancy termination.

Her eyes locked on the last three words, and her heart started to pound. She scrolled through several pages to the doctor's notes.

27-year-old female presented in ED after waking up this morning with 101.4 fever, severe abdominal and back pain, persistent and heavy vaginal bleeding of two sanitary pads an hour for previous 6 hours. Recent onset nausea and vomiting. Patient's friend reports patient received elective termination of 7- week pregnancy two days ago with no complications at that time.

Height: 5'4"
Weight: 152lbs
*Diagnosis: Incomplete elective pregnancy termination and
post infection*

Kara's hands slid from the keyboard in disbelief. She re-read the diagnosis again.

Incomplete elective pregnancy termination.

Rachel Graves. An abortion.
Unbelievable.
Every crazy rumor and theory she'd heard about Rachel's abrupt departure years ago didn't seem so crazy anymore.

She re-read the file again and again, picking up new details each time. The height and weight seemed grossly inaccurate. She knew Rachel was closer to six foot. Tall and slender. Strange that the nurse noted it incorrectly.

A woman from the billing department walked by and Kara quickly minimized her computer screen. Confidentiality laws were strict. She shouldn't have even opened the medical file as soon as she recognized the name. She should have passed the request to Val to handle.

But she had opened it. And read it without hesitation.

Alone again, Kara maximized the screen, hands shaking, and emailed the reports to the requesting gynecology office. She shut down her computer, gathered her purse, and left.

As she navigated the rush hour traffic, Kara couldn't stop thinking about beautiful, perfect Rachel who had lived rent-free in Kara's mind as this unattainable standard.

Traffic halted suddenly, and Kara slammed on the brakes, nearly rear-ending an SUV. Reading the chart had rattled her beyond the mere shock of discovering Rachel's secret.

Because before she met Paul, Kara herself had gotten pregnant.

She'd been living with the junkie boyfriend in a roach-infested apartment on the south side and neither had jobs.

To support their habits, they shoplifted and returned items for cash. When she discovered she was pregnant, she was already eight weeks along and shooting three hundred dollars' worth of heroin into her arms daily.

It hadn't even been a decision, really. More like an act of mercy.

She'd called her brother, a doctor, and he'd sent his wife, also a doctor, to take her to a clinic and pay for the procedure.

Paul had listened sympathetically to the stories about her past—the drugs, the terrible boyfriends, the lies, the crimes—and without judgement. She wasn't that person anymore, he would say, after she revealed each story. She was an inspiration. Her fight to turn her life around and find God was one of the things he loved most about her.

But, she'd never told him about the pregnancy.

Kara turned the car onto Paul's street and took the corner too sharply, clipping the curb with a jolt.

It was her last secret. The final admission to make before they walked down the aisle and took their vows next spring. She should've told him sooner, but she couldn't bring herself to say the words out loud. Not because she regretted her decision, but because she was afraid Paul's nonjudgement might have a limit.

No. He would love her anyway, she kept telling herself. She wasn't that person anymore, just like he'd said.

But she *was* that person, wasn't she? Those days were still part of her cloth, no matter how much she tried to bleach it.

She entered Paul's parents' house through the unlocked garage door and removed her shoes. Cabinets banged, and a spicy, warm aroma drifted from the kitchen. Kara walked into the spacious room on silent, bare feet. Paul was bent over a pan at the stove. He touched a large spoon of red sauce to his lips.

"Hi," she finally said.

Paul straightened and turned around. He looked handsome as he always did in designer jeans and a crisp polo shirt.

"Hi, yourself," he said.

Kara moved toward him, and he lightly kissed her cheek.

She sat down at the table and clutched her purse to her chest. "Smells good," she said.

"Hope you're hungry." He stirred the noodles with a pasta spoon, then studied her for a moment. "You look tired. Hard day?"

Kara shrugged. "No. I don't know…" She wasn't sure how to label her feelings at that moment.

Paul turned the burner down and checked a loaf of bread in the oven. He sat in the chair next to her and gathered her hands in his own. He began talking about his day, but Kara couldn't concentrate. All she could think about was Rachel's chart, the stark black and white words across the computer screen, and what Paul might say if he knew what Rachel had done.

Like a test.

Her cheeks grew hot.

"Are you sure you're alright?" Paul asked.

Kara shook her head. She was sweating now, and for the first time in months, that old urge to slide a needle into her skin itched deep in her gut.

She knew it was illegal to repeat what she'd read in Rachel's chart. She could lose her job if someone found out. She would never be able to work in healthcare again, and with her addictive past, jobs were already hard to get.

But Rachel's secret felt like a gift, like a toe dipped in the water to check the temperature before Kara dove in headfirst with her own confession.

She cleared her throat and spoke quietly. "Actually, something did happen at work today."

Paul released her hands and leaned back in the chair.

"I got a request for a record," she said, "for someone I know. Someone we both know."

His brow wrinkled. "Really? Who?"

She hugged the coat closer. "It was an emergency room report for Rachel. From a few weeks ago in July."

"Rachel Graves?" His brow lifted in surprise. "At the county hospital?"

Kara nodded. "She went there with an infection. She'd had a procedure and there were minor complications."

"What kind of procedure?" Paul straightened.

Kara drew a deep breath and the words tumbled out. "It was an elective termination of a pregnancy. An…an abortion."

Paul's face remained expressionless. He stared hard at Kara's mouth for a long moment. The scent of burning tomatoes filled the room. He calmly rose, returned to the stove, and picked up the wooden spoon to stir the sauce.

Kara's mind scrambled. She started to worry he was disgusted with her breach in confidentiality. The itch grew stronger. She started babbling to fill the silence. "I, I know I'm not supposed to repeat what I read at work, but I'm telling you because we all care about Rachel, and she's our friend." She paused, that tight grip growing in her stomach. "I, I'm only telling you because I think she could use some prayers right now." She said it knowing it was a flimsy excuse.

Kara stopped talking and waited.

Paul carefully set the spoon down and turned around. His face was complaisant, the lines around his mouth soft. Kara couldn't read his expression. Was he angry? Upset? She still couldn't tell.

Paul crossed his arms over his chest. "What a whore," he finally said.

Her throat tightened. "What?"

He leaned against the counter, his posture relaxed. "I'm sorry, but she is." He shook his head. "She'll burn in eternal hell."

Paul sat back down, gathered her hands again, and stared gently into her eyes.

She'd known at some point in their relationship, hadn't she? Deep down? She'd seen a glimpse of this other side of him, once, during an argument about how much he disliked her sister-in-law—a successful doctor—and how she needed to "learn her place" in her marriage. At the time, Kara had chosen to ignore it. To forget about the comment altogether and forge ahead with this life. Until now.

"I'm so glad you told me," Paul said.

Slowly, Kara withdrew her hands from him and stood. She reached for her coat and slipped the strap of her purse over her shoulder. Slid her feet into her shoes.

"I'm so glad I told you, too," she said.

The Revisionary

Rachel Graves's new client was FUCC, Families United Christ Church, and the first thing she needed to discuss with the board was their acronym. How so many members had never noticed (or said something, anything) was beyond her.

She arrived at the classic seventies style stone façade building a short drive away from her Hyatt hotel near the St. Louis Arch and entered a dingy vestibule. Next to the main doors sat a side table cluttered with dozens of ugly paper fliers for a mother's group, Wednesday night Bible study, and an Easter egg hunt from last April even though it was now July.

She paused at a placard affixed to the wall: FUCC WELCOMES YOU!

Oh, dear.

She tapped her phone screen, opened the voice memo app, and recorded her first impressions.

This job might take a while.

She followed the too-small signs to the church offices but found the half-dozen cubicles empty. She checked the clock on her phone. Five minutes past her meeting time with Pastor Dennis Moore, the head pastor who had contracted her company to help with an increasingly shrinking attendance and membership.

Rachel's job at Revisionaries, Inc. was to help businesses and organizations identify issues affecting their growth and public perceptions. Because she'd been raised in her family's similarly conservative church, her boss figured she still knew this world well and specifically assigned her this client.

She searched two more dead end hallways before finally locating a single door marked *Pastor*. She juggled her thick binder in one hand and with her other, snapped a quick picture on her phone of the labyrinth hall systems and more confusing signage.

Whenever she worked with a new client, she spent time observing, talking with focus groups, examining logos, building up print and digital assets, and conducting team building exercises. Her specialties were websites, social media, and leadership issues. At the end of her two weeks on site, she would make targeted recommendations for the organization to re-brand and start attracting growth again. It all sounded a bit boring, but Rachel had flourished in the work.

Rachel continued down the hall and found a cramped conference room with a table way too big for the space. When she peeked her head into a small office next to it, she was surprised to find it empty except for a teenage girl sitting on a lone metal folding chair in the corner, shoes off, legs crisscrossed, with a sketch pad open on her lap. She bent intently over the page, a pencil audibly scratching across the paper.

"Excuse me," Rachel said.

The girl looked up.

"I'm looking for Pastor Moore," Rachel said. "Do you know where I can find him?"

"He's at the post office," The girl answered. "He'll be back in a few minutes."

Rachel entered and extended her hand. "My name's Rachel. I'm the—"

"I know who you are," the girl said. She laid her pencil down, but didn't shake Rachel's hand.

Rachel stood awkwardly. Closer, she saw the girl was sketching a cartoon version of an older man with an exaggerated nose, ears, and hair.

"My uncle," the girl said, gesturing to the picture. "He's the pastor. He hates it when I draw him."

"It's very good. What's your name?"

"Kelly. I do real portraits, too." She picked up the pencil and added more shading to the thinning crown of hair. "But these are way more fun."

"You're really talented."

The girl tipped her head to the side and studied Rachel. "I could draw you, if you like."

Rachel smiled. "That would be fun." She paused, glancing around the empty room again. "Are you waiting in here for someone?"

Kelly's expression tightened and she looked back down at the picture. "No," she said. "I'm being punished."

"Oh. What for?"

Kelly ran her index finger around the outline of the hair, creating wispy smudges. "My mom caught me partying and smoking weed, so she sent me here for my aunt and the pastor to . . . " she paused to make exaggerated air quotes, "straighten me out." She shook her head and laughed, an angry, rueful sound. "My mom doesn't know shit."

Before Rachel could say more, the door suddenly swung open and Pastor Dennis Moore, or "Pastor D" as the congregants called him, entered. Rachel recognized him from the photo on the outdated FUCC website.

"Miss Groves?" he said sharply, looking almost angry to see her in there.

"It's Graves, but please call me Rachel." She offered him a quick handshake.

He glanced at Kelly, the unflattering sketch of himself, and wordlessly snatched the sketch pad out of her hands. He then left the small office.

Rachel followed as Pastor D firmly closed the door behind them, removed a keyring from his pocket, and locked the knob. "My niece," he said. "She's staying here this summer to spend time in meditation with God. No distractions." He turned back to Rachel, his face suddenly brightening, and said, "Let's talk in my office."

Rachel followed him down the hall, troubled by what she'd just seen and heard, but fixed to mind her own business.

Inside, his office was cluttered with wall-to-ceiling sagging shelves of books and boxes stacked in every corner marked by years. Old paper sermons, she guessed, just like the pastor at her parents' church in West Des Moines.

Pastor D tossed the sketch pad into the garbage. "You look too young to do this job," he said. "And far too pretty." He smiled broadly as his gaze slowly swept her from head to toe and uncomfortably lingered at her chest.

Rachel didn't respond and instead pressed her mouth into a firm line. She got that sometimes while working—she looked so young for her age, she was so tall and pretty she should model, blah, blah, blah—and it always irritated her. She'd earned her double business and marketing degrees with honors and had the best client-improvement record at Revisionaries. For five years, she'd worked with dozens of organizations and successfully improved their marketing strategies and client growth by an average of ten to fifteen percent. And it had nothing to do with her age or being "pretty." All things she would've liked to snap back at Pastor D but held her tongue like a professional.

"At any rate," Pastor D said, "I'm excited to work with you."

He sat in the chair behind his imposing, dark wood desk and Rachel was forced to sit in one of the chairs facing him, as if she were in the principal's office.

"Well," Pastor D started, "like I told you on the phone, FUCC was established over sixty years ago."

He said the letters of the acronym, F-U-C-C, proving her hunch that everyone was so used to saying F-U-C-C that they'd failed to notice what the FUCC it actually spelled.

Rachel nodded. "Yes, right away I noticed your—"

"Shortly after I transferred here as head pastor last year," he cut her off, "we started to experience membership decline. Some of it was aging members dying, young people moving away and whatnot."

"Which according to my market research many churches experience—"

"But nothing we've done since then has made a difference," he interrupted again. "So, here you are."

Rachel paused before answering this time to ensure he was done speaking. "Here I am," she finally said. "Right away I noted that your church shares a few key characteristics and challenges as several of my past clients I've successfully worked with, so I'm confident I can create an effective turnaround strategy."

"That's what we're hoping," he said, and she caught his gaze as it once again flickered from her face to her chest.

Now her internal antenna went up. Was the guy just a creep, or something worse?

Rachel opened her binder and handed him their introductory information packet and schedule for the next week. After wrapping up the meeting, she asked for a full tour of the church.

He walked her through the usual—the sanctuary and fellowship hall (no notes on those spaces as they looked good, inviting and functional), the tiny classrooms (could use a little brightening and better configuration), and the nursery (very outdated and was likely unappealing to new parents).

No acknowledgement of the niece when they passed the empty office.

"As you can see," Pastor D said, "one of our biggest challenges is classrooms and large group gathering spaces."

She snapped more pictures on her phone.

"We have quite a bit of unused space in our basement, though," he said. "I'd like to show it to you and tell you my plans for it."

He unlocked the door, and Rachel followed him down a set of dark, narrow stairs, already noting she'd never recommend using this basement for anything because the stairwell alone was dangerous and not handicapped accessible. But she went down into the dank-smelling bowels because her job required her to be accommodating and affable at all times, a good way to keep clients happy. And happy clients were more likely to listen to her.

At the bottom of the stairs, Pastor D flicked on a single overhead light that barely illuminated the claustrophobic space.

"So, you see there's some real untapped potential down here," he said.

"Possibly," Rachel answered, stepping over several dead spiders sprinkled across the concrete floor like morbid confetti. "I'll keep this in mind." (To forget.)

"I would love to start a movie club," Pastor D said. "This space could be perfect for it. Show a wholesome family movie a couple times a month. Set up some folding chairs, put a TV over there." He pointed to a moldy cinderblock wall with peeling paint.

"Hmm," she replied, unable to bring herself to say more.

A few months ago, she'd dealt with a similar client. An older male CEO of a small, failing family company who was full of his own "ideas," and from the start didn't take kindly to a younger person—a younger *woman*—giving any recommendations, even though he'd been the one to hire her. She'd figured out the most effective way to deal with and keep him engaged in the process was to ask questions.

Lots and lots of questions, even when she already knew the answers. That way he felt, from the beginning, like a wealth of knowledge and authority on everything. In other words, like her superior.

She launched this strategy with Pastor D and the more questions she asked, the more animated he became, her approach clearly working.

As she made a few notes in her phone, she felt him staring at her again.

"Do you have a boyfriend?"

Now the internal antennae turned into a blaring alarm and Rachel stiffened. "No, I don't. Right now, I'm just focused on my career."

Pastor D shook his head. "You career girls. Just don't wait too long and dry up." He winked and then laughed loudly.

Rachel ignored his comment and checked the time on her phone. "Why don't we head back upstairs and talk a little about the layout of the church offices?"

"After you." He held his hand out for her to go first. As she started up the stairs, he switched off the light, plunging them into darkness. She stumbled on a step.

"Whoa, there," Pastor D said, and briefly but firmly, cupped her right ass cheek with his hand.

Rachel froze.

Maybe she'd imagined it.

But no.

She'd felt his thick, warm hand cup and squeeze for a second.

Regaining her grip on the handrail, she quickly ascended the rest of the steps well ahead of him.

At the top, they stepped into the harsh fluorescent lights of the hallway. Pastor D continued chatting as if nothing had happened.

"I also have more ideas for our summer Bible camp I'd like to talk to you about," he said. "And some young adult programming."

"Great," Rachel answered flatly, a knot tightening in her chest.

SIX DAYS LATER, RACHEL SAT at the desk in her hotel room squinting out the window at the sunrise reflecting off the metal façade of the sweeping Arch. She turned back to her computer and refreshed her email, but there was still no reply from her boss. Refreshed again. Nothing. She sighed.

FUCC was officially the most difficult client she'd worked with. Pastor D had resisted every step of the process. He'd been defensive of the church name (claiming no one else saw a problem with the acronym) and outdated website (which he had designed, she learned). He'd bristled at her recommendation to restage the vestibule (her questions strategy quickly breaking down by day two), and resisted letting her talk to focus groups (finally relenting and allowing her to interview a mere two congregants when normally she interviewed over a dozen, plus non-congregant community members to get outside perceptions). But he'd become downright argumentative when she'd gently voiced her concerns about the movie nights in the dreadful basement and a realistic re-enactment of Christ's crucifixion at Bible camp in a few weeks that would include hanging an adult parishioner on a cross.

Male board members seemed afraid to speak up about differing opinions, and the women barely spoke at all. Except for Pastor D's wife, Kathy, the head of the board (in a blatant conflict of interest) who enthusiastically agreed with everything that came out of her husband's mouth. There were endless squabbles in the women's group and steering committee, and just since Rachel had arrived, another young family had resigned as members, leaving a critical childcare vacancy in the nursery.

But that list was the least of her challenges.

Unable to sleep last night, she'd finally sent an email to her boss at Revisionaries with the subject line: *Serious Issues with New Client.*

In the message, she'd crafted a full account of what she'd been dealing with all week.

First, the ass grab in the basement. Asking if she was a real blonde. A disgusting joke about women's periods. A bizarre story about how when he was in high school, he had a reputation for such being a ladies' man he'd been nicknamed "Dennis the Menace." Then leaning over her shoulder to "read" a computer screen while obviously looking down her shirt. A deliberate arm brush across her chest when he reached for a paper, in full view of the church administrator, an older woman who showed no reaction. Laying his hand on her knee beneath the table while they were sitting in the conference during a board meeting.

All escalating to the incident in the kitchen yesterday afternoon.

And in the midst of all this, the niece was locked in the empty room for eight hours every day. Rachel saw Pastor D escort Kelly inside at eight a.m., allow her a bathroom break at noon, and escort her out of the building at four p.m.

No one acknowledged her presence behind the door. Not the administrator, assistant pastor, custodian, or anyone from the board. It was as if the locked door and girl behind it didn't exist.

But Rachel knew she was there. Each day, she'd checked the knob, and each day it was locked, and whenever she pressed her ear to the door, she could hear small noises from inside. A cough. The squeak of the chair. Feet shuffling across carpet.

And each day that passed, Rachel was more confounded, more disturbed, until finally two days ago, she'd entered the women's restroom during the lunch hour and heard someone in a stall vomiting.

Rachel waited by the sink. The toilet flushed, and Kelly emerged looking pale.

"Hi," Rachel said quietly.

Kelly said nothing and turned on a faucet. She bent to sip the water, swish, and spit it out.

"Are you okay?" Rachel asked.

Kelly shrugged and compressed the soap dispenser over and over until a creamy mound formed in her palm. She stared at the pearl blob, unmoving. Finally, she blinked, rubbed her hands together, and rinsed her hands. She turned to Rachel, and slowly, silently shook her head back and forth. Then, she put a wet finger to her lips, soapy water dripping down her wrists, and pointed to the door.

"Tell me what's going on," Rachel whispered. "Maybe I can help."

Kelly stared at her with the faucet still running, as if scrutinizing Rachel for something. Finally, she reached for a paper towel, dried her hands, and gestured for Rachel to move closer. She pressed her lips to Rachel's ear and told her, in a rush of words, the entire story.

The following day in the bathroom, they'd made a plan.

Rachel refreshed her email for the third time. Finally, a reply from her boss. She quickly scanned the message.

Hey Rach,

Wow, I'm so sorry for what you've been dealing with. This is totally unacceptable, and I'll terminate our contract with the church immediately. Cancel your remaining meetings with them, and I'll send an email to the pastor and board members with our termination document. I already filled it out and attached it here for you to review and add your digital signature below mine. I'll then email it once you're safely on the road heading back to Minneapolis.

Let me know if there's anything else I can do to help you in the meantime.

Jessie

Rachel clicked on the attached PDF and read the document. Jessie had checked the box *Termination for cause due to client's actions or inactions*, and filled in the explanation with a literal copy and paste of Rachel's email detailing the issues with Pastor D.

Step one of their plan, done.

She started typing her reply.

Hey Jessie,

Thanks for the support and quick plan of action. I'm packing up my things now, but I need to go to the church to collect some things before I leave. I'll email the signed contract once I'm ready to get on the road, and then you can send it on to the church.

See you soon,
Rach

That would be step two.

As Rachel added her digital signature, her gaze lingered on the tag line and the company mission statement in the header of the document.

Revise your potential.

In a way, it was what Rachel had been doing in her own life for the past few years. She'd dared to see her life and future differently than what her parents and other people around her had wanted or expected.

Revision. To see differently.

Revise your potential.

Sometimes, it felt like she'd had to walk through fire to build this different life, to realize her potential. She'd dealt with so many versions of "Pastor Ds" in her old life and already knew how this would play out. The denials, the blame, the name-calling. Liar. Temptress. Whore.

She'd learned the hard way to document everything. Screenshots of nasty text messages. Audio recordings of the screaming. A single picture of the bruise on her arm from a fight, when she'd finally ended the relationship.

She'd gotten out alive, gotten away, and started over. Sometimes, she wondered if she should warn the new woman in his life, the new fiancé. Sometimes, she wondered if the new fiancé would find out the hard way, like she did, and make the same choice to leave and start over.

Revision. To see differently.

It's what Rachel had told Kelly in the bathroom. *You can always start over. Revise a new story for yourself. I can help you do that.*

Rachel opened a new message to Jessie and attached the signed termination document along with a video file she'd uploaded to her laptop last night. Then, she saved the email to her draft folder and finished packing her things.

AT THE CHURCH, RACHEL PARKED her car at the side entrance and quietly entered. She quickly made her way down the empty hall to the small office door. There, she slipped a flathead screwdriver from her purse she'd purchased at a hardware store last night and began to carefully remove the screws to the knob, twisting them out slowly, one at a time. When the last screw slid from the hole, she gently guided the knob out and pushed the door open.

Kelly immediately emerged and they hurried down the hallway together.

Outside, they got into Rachel's car, and drove away.

THIRTY MINUTES OUTSIDE OF ST. LOUIS, Rachel pulled over at a gas station and tapped "send" on the saved email with the termination contract and a video file attached. A video Rachel had secretly recorded while she was in the kitchen washing a plate late yesterday afternoon. As she predicted, he'd entered the kitchen, come up close behind her to set a mug in the basin, pressed his erect penis against her back, and said, leaning into her neck, "Is the dirty girl washing dirty dishes?" When she'd startled and quickly moved away, he'd laughed, calling her "so jumpy," and acted as if he hadn't done anything.

The video and audio were perfectly clear.

She'd cc'd every member of the church and a reporter from the *St. Louis Dispatch* on the email.

In the passenger seat, Kelly flipped to another page in the new sketch book Rachel had also purchased for her last night, along with a few clothes and toiletries, to reveal a cartoon version of Rachel with a large head, exaggerated eyes and lips, her name in fat, puffy letters at the bottom.

"I hope you don't mind," Kelly said.

Rachel laughed. "I love it."

Kelly tore out the page and handed it to Rachel.

"You have to sign it, though," Rachel said.

Kelly smiled and scribbled in the bottom right corner, then held it out again:

from one Revisionary to another

Caricatures

At the west end of the Grand Concourse of the Iowa State Fairgrounds, beneath a large tent in the early morning August humidity, I remove the canvas cover from my table and open my case of markers and Prismacolor Color Sticks. It's day two of the ten-day fair, and usually the busiest of the weekend. The other artists begin to arrive and set up their spaces. We chat amiably through yawns, clutching cups and mugs of coffee, or paper plates of greasy breakfast food from nearby vendors. My friend and fellow artist Frankie stretches her arms overhead, her loose shirt lifting to reveal the edge of a floral tattoo scrolling up her side into her rib cage like some sort of trellis vine.

"God," she sighs, "I fucking hate this humidity. Don't you? It's like trying to breathe vapor." She drops her arms and sags into her camping chair. "I need a beer."

I laugh. "It's only eight in the morning."

"All the more reason."

The west gates of the grounds open, and fairgoers begin to straggle through. The first hour is always slow, but by mid-morning every artist under our tent is busy doing portraits.

My specialty is giant heads and faces with happy bubble letter names of the subject at the bottom. I seem to mostly attract kids and young people, while Frankie, who does full cartoon bodies, seems to attract more couples. Over the past eight years, I'd gathered a nice following on social media and a regular spot at the state fair. With big fairs and festivals, I always set the goal to average roughly ten minutes per drawing. It's art, but also commerce, and time is money.

A few hours and several portraits later, I have a break and use the time to eat a quick snack: a chocolate pudding cup and granola bar my boyfriend packed for me. Jamie's always looking out for me like that. As I eat, I watch throngs of people pass by on the congested Grand Concourse. A few yards away from our tent, a long line has already formed in front of an insanely popular chocolate chip cookie vendor that sells cups or whole bucketfuls.

Two women enter our tent holding hands and sit at Frankie's station, giggling.

"I've always wanted to do one of these," the first woman says.

Frankie introduces herself and helps position them in front of her plain blue backdrop.

"I'm Hailey," the first woman says, "and this is my wife, Jessie."

The woman named Jessie laughs. "I'm still getting used to that word. We just got married last month but we knew each other as kids."

"Congratulations," Frankie answers. "Why don't I make you brides in your portrait?"

"Yes!" Jessie claps her hands. "I love it!"

I listen to the conversation and smile. Jamie and I knew each other as kids, too, when we rode the same school bus for one year. We crossed paths once again when we were teens, during a party for my younger sister, though we didn't speak. Jamie likes to tease me that I ignored him and sat in the corner with my nose in my sketch pad the whole time, which sounds like something I would've done at that age.

My phone dings with a text from Jamie's sister.

Will you and J be at the fam reunion in the Ozarks over Labor Day weekend?

I send her a thumb's up emoji, and type, Be there Thurs eve and leave Mon morn

She immediately hearts it and replies, E and N there Fri eve with the baby til Sun

I'd also known Lacey as a child, on that same bus route, when we were seatmates. Her testimony about our time together on the school bus became critical during the trial.

I finish my granola bar and throw the wrapper away. Next to me, Frankie sketches as she keeps chatting with the couple, asking them friendly questions, as we all do to get a sense of their personalities to help inform the picture.

"We're here visiting my parents for the weekend," Hailey says, "but we just bought a house in St. Paul."

"St. Paul's a fun city," Frankie says.

"I *love* the neighborhood," Jessie adds.

"Oh, my God, so much better than your old neighborhood." Hailey clicks her tongue. Jessie agrees.

I lean my head back against my chair, feeling drowsy from the heat and hum of happy chatter. By noon everyone will be sweating through their clothes and trying to seek shade and a breeze wherever they can find it.

I doze off for a second when a familiar voice jolts me awake.

"Are you available to do a picture?"

My eyes snap open, and I lift my head.

I haven't seen her since I testified at the trial five years ago. I'm surprised by the gray streaks in her hair, the fine lines around her mouth, and crevices deeply etched across her forehead. She clutches a brown purse at her side, her hands anxiously clasped at her belly.

I stare at her for a long moment, considering what to do. Ignore her. Tell her to leave. Get up and walk away. I could go into the Varied Industries building. Get in the air conditioning for a few minutes, absorbed in the shoulder-to-shoulder crowds, anywhere she isn't.

But to my own surprise, I gesture to the empty stool in front of my table. "Sure," I say, my voice flat. "Whatever."

She steps around the stool and sits stiffly on the edge, now clutching the purse on her lap, as if for protection. From me, I'm sure. A breeze flaps my smudgy gray cloth backdrop behind her and ruffles the lacy collar of her ugly top.

I slap a piece of fresh white paper onto my board, clip it into place, and start silently outlining with a fresh black Sharpie. I feel Frankie side-eye me, but I ignore her and focus on drawing broad, thick strokes, creating an excessively fat head, big ears, and a long bulbous nose.

My subject clears her throat. "How are you? You look well."

I ignore her comment and draw small, beady eyes, like a vulture.

"How's Martha?"

I pause at this, my hand trembling, jaw painfully clenched. I want to say she lost the right to ask about us a long time ago.

Again, I ignore her question. Instead, I take a deep breath through my nose, and resume sketching without looking at her. I know every detail of her face from memory. The tiny scar above her eye from a cat scratch. The large freckle on her left cheek. How her thin lips disappear when she smiles.

But I don't know why I let her sit.

I try to think about Jamie and the gentle way he always kisses the top of my head when he enters a room.

"I saw on your Instagram you would be here," the subject says. "You've gotten really good."

My eyes burn from concentrating so hard on the paper. My skin turns clammy despite the heat. I've made so much progress in recent years with intense therapy, my art, and reconnecting with Jamie and his family, who treat me like their own. I hate myself for coming undone in a matter of minutes by this subject's presence.

I pause to gather myself. Crack my knuckles one at a time as I gaze, once again, at the ever-growing line for cookies.

Frankie finishes the black and white portion of her sketch and starts filling in color. She drew the women with big doe eyes, flowing wedding veils, and heart-shaped lips. All exaggerations of what a good caricature artist sees before them: the surface, the external presentation people curate for the rest of the world.

Sometimes, I observe strangers in passing and get a brief vision of the caricature I would draw for them. I focus on something specific. An impish grin. A pert nose. Thin, stern lips. But then I wonder, does the person have an impish personality? Is the person pert? Stern?

I've had my own caricature portrait drawn by fellow artists many times, and it's always some version of a badass. Hard looking. Angry. Don't fuck with me. My curated surface, I assume.

But that's not at all how I think of myself, though. I don't know how I would draw my own caricature.

"Do you want me to go?" The subject asks, and when I glance at her, she looks like she might start crying at any moment.

I re-focus on the picture, and to my surprise, answer, "No." I start sketching again, giving her a sagging, wrinkly neck even though she doesn't have one.

The air has grown hotter, thicker in the mere minutes since the subject sat down. She is sweating from the heat—or from my presence, I hope—and wipes her temples. Because of this, I add a few drops of perspiration in the wrinkles of her brow, give her limp, flat hair that sticks to her forehead.

The newlywed couple is still chatting about their wedding and new house while Frankie shades in their gauzy white veils. She pauses and looks at my picture as I'm adding horns to the woman's head, then looks at me, and quietly asks, "Bruh, are you okay?"

"I'm fine," I answer.

The subject hears this exchange between me and Frankie and says, "I don't want to upset you. I just wanted to see you. That you're okay."

I slap the marker down on my sketch board and look straight into her eyes for the first time. "I'm okay *now*," I say. "No thanks to you."

Finally, the tears spill, running down her cheeks and dripping off the end of her chin, onto the front of her ugly shirt. "I'm so sorry," she whispers. "I made so many mistakes."

"I don't care," I say.

She swipes her nose with the back of her hand. "I should've believed you. You're my daughter and no matter what—"

"Stop talking." I stare at her shoes. Blue and white Sketcher walking shoes I recognize, and this enrages me even more because they're the same damn shoes she was wearing when she left me at the church—the prison—with *him*. When she cried in a pathetic, weepy voice, *Maybe you can straighten her out. I'm done trying!*

My subject presses her hand to her chest, her voice quivering with more tears. "I should've never left you there. Kathy convinced me you were lying. That he was going to help you."

"Stop crying," I hiss.

Now the couple glances at us, along with Frankie.

"I wanted to talk to you . . ." she hiccups a little sob, "after your testimony, or even after the sentencing, but . . ." She looks down at her hands and shakes her head. "I was too ashamed."

I want to punch her in the face. Kick her in the gut. Stomp on those fucking shoes.

Instead, I shift my gaze back to the passing crowd, at people cooling themselves with fans on sticks advertising community colleges and a local radio station, and calmly ask, "Do you want color added to your picture?"

My subject takes a long time to answer. "Yes, thank you," she finally says.

From my box of color sticks, I select dark reds, blues, and an ugly brown I never use because it's the color of shit. As I fill in the hair and sharp, pointy horns, I try to think about something else. Someone else. I think about *her*.

I haven't thought about her in a long time. What she did for me. The plan she came up with to get me out of the locked room in the church, to get me away from my family. I think about how her secret video, shared hundreds of times across social media, opened the floodgates for other girls to come forward with similar experiences. How she brought me here, to the other side of this city, to her parents' house, where I stayed in a pretty room with the softest bed I'd ever slept in, and how she slept in her childhood room across the hall with posters of a boy band still hanging on the walls. How she held my hand at the clinic during the procedure, and during the cramping and fever a few days later. How she stayed so calm while she drove to a hospital emergency room, and handed me her insurance card without a single word, and how I understood and silently accepted it.

After I got better, she helped me find a safe place to stay. Told me to start over. To see differently.

Her.

The right person at the right time.

I wonder if I'll ever see her again. Sometimes when I watch the crowds on the Grand Concourse, I look for her. She's so tall and pretty, easy to spot. But I've never seen her.

Frankie has finished the couple's portrait, and Bailey exclaims they look so happy in the picture. Jessie says it's because they *are* happy.

They leave, still holding hands.

I finish shading the colors in my portrait, and add my subject's first name in big, sharp block letters beneath. Then I unclip the paper, turn it around, and show her.

She's not crying anymore. She silently stares at it.

Frankie stares, too. I can literally feel her holding her breath, shocked at the picture I've drawn.

"I love it," my subject says. "How much do I owe you?"

"One fifty," I say.

She nods and unzips her purse, an drab shit brown, the same color I've shaded her hair in the picture. She removes a wallet, counts out two hundred dollars in twenties, and hands the stack to me. I tuck it into the money bag in my satchel near my feet.

"Will you please sign it?" she says.

I uncap my black sharpie and scribble in the right-hand corner.

The Revisionary

I hand the portrait back to her, and she turns to leave.

"Wait," I say.

She stops. The edges of the portrait flutter in the breeze.

"You could . . . I guess . . ." But I'm not sure exactly what I want to tell her. Finally, I say, "You can message me. Through my Instagram. If you want."

She smiles, and just like I remembered, her thin lips curl over her teeth and disappear. "Thank you. I'd like that."

I watch the back of her head as she walks out of the tent and onto the Grand Concourse, until the crowd swallows her, and she disappears.

"What . . ." Frankie says under her breath, "the *ever-loving fuck* was that about?"

"Nothing," I answer.

My tone must convey a warning, and Frankie heeds it. She leans back in her chair and opens her phone screen.

A teenage girl enters the tent and shyly approaches my table. "Are you the one who does the faces with the names?" she asks.

I finally look away from the crowd, blink, collect myself. "I am," I say and gesture to my chair.

"Oh, good." She sits down. She wears a tight crop top and carries an enormous yellow Stanley cup. Her bright pink acrylic nails are ridiculously long, too big for her slender fingers, and I've already seen so many versions of her at this fair. Just different colors of the cup. She tells me her name and starts answering my questions about how old she is, where she lives, what activities she enjoys. But I still need something more, something below the surface.

She smiles, and there it is. A genuinely sweet, insecure smile that exposes a subtle gap between her front teeth, and soft crinkles around her eyes.

I know how I'll draw her.

I pick up my black marker.

I begin again.

Hyatt Pune

I.

Tricia can't sleep. She arrived in Pune, a sprawling city in western India, over twenty-four hours ago, and despite the exhausting travel, she's only dozed a few minutes. She lays awake in the plush hotel bed, tossing, turning, kicking the duvet, punching and flipping the pillows, getting so close to the very edge of sleep, but never quite dropping over it.

Just before five a.m., a full day ahead of home in Minneapolis, she gives up and rises. Dresses in khaki slacks and a plain polo shirt.

Today, she'll be working at a small clinic a few blocks south of her hotel. She takes a fifteen-minute car ride that's a lesson in anarchy. Her driver for the week, Mahesh, is friendly, and chats about his six-month-old daughter who has a rash on her little butt cheeks. Tricia tells him to try a certain brand of diaper ointment and to take her to the pediatrician if the rash hasn't improved after three days. As they talk, he steers his battered silver Toyota in, out, and around the dizzying mash of traffic, constantly beeping his horn.

The jerky motions, spine-jolting potholes, choking fumes, and relentless noise make Tricia so nauseous she turns to long-forgotten Lamaze breathing just to keep from puking in the back seat.

THE *HEALING HANDS* CLINIC is an unremarkable office tucked into the corner of a strip mall that from the outside looks like it could be a cheap massage parlor. It's stocked with minimal medical supplies and old equipment, and she works alongside Dr. Rajesh, her dearest friend from medical school days in Chicago. Last year, Raj invited her to register with the Medical Council of India to do some pro bono dermatology work with him in Pune. She liked the idea of philanthropic services and decided a week in early November was a good time to do it, when the girls' activities hit a lull.

While Raj, a cardiologist, sees heart patients, Tricia treats a variety of common skin issues like dermatitis, psoriasis, eczema, and hives, but also a rainbow of fungal and bacterial infections, and the largest abscess she's ever seen. It reminds her of the massive abscess on Jay's sister's arm many years ago—at that time the largest she'd ever treated—before Kara got clean.

By mid-morning, the line for Tricia's services stretches out the clinic door and wraps around the corner. She gets barely ten minutes for her lunch break—an egg and cheese sandwich Raj brought her—before she is back at it.

The physical fatigue, she's hopeful, will finally put her to sleep tonight.

At the end of the long day, she has dinner with Raj, his lovely wife Geetha, and their precocious boy, Ahmed. She eats delicious tandoori chicken and naan, sips a warm tea Geetha says will help her sleep. Ahmed tells her to count sheep. She plays chess with him, and he beats her.

II.

Tricia still can't sleep. Geetha's tea has not helped. Ahmed's counting sheep has not helped. She takes a prescription sleeping pill, meditates, and reads a boring novel until her eyes burn, but nothing helps.

It is two in the morning Pune time, and her mind will not surrender. It just keeps turning, turning, turning, the pill having no effect. She thinks about her girls at school, about Jay at the hospital, her entire life twelve hours behind her, still in the middle of their day.

And she thinks about stupid things, like her hairdresser getting divorced, the inconvenient temporary road closure in front of her gym, the leaky sink faucet in their kitchen. But also important things, like Jay asking his sister to help with the girls while Tricia is gone; Kara, who's been clean since a brief relapse after breaking up with a prick fiancé years ago. But Tricia still worries.

She sits up in bed and rips the silky black sleep mask from her eyes, switches on the lamp. She squints, opens her phone screen, and taps a music app to search for sleep sounds. She selects a playlist for "gentle rain," takes a melatonin tablet, and texts the girls.

Tricia: How's it going with Aunt Kara?

Lydia: good we swam in the indoor pool at her apartment today

Claudia: when is my next braces apt???? I have a lose wire

Tricia: Monday. It's on the calendar.

Not only is Claudia's next orthodontist appointment on the shared family calendar, it's also on the three-page list of instructions and other vital information she created for Jay and the girls, none of whom read it with any attention.

Tricia waits, staring at the screen—absorbing all that blue light she knows she shouldn't—waiting for a reply. The rippling bubbles appear a few minutes later.

Claudia: kk

Tricia sends a thumbs up, but slaps her phone face down on the nightstand in annoyance. She's halfway around the world while Jay is just across town, and yet she still gets the texts and questions. She sinks back into the mound of pillows and closes her eyes to the sound of gentle rain falling.

She doesn't sleep.

RAJ SENDS TRICIA TO WORK at an orphanage in another part of the city. B.S.S.K., though she doesn't know what the letters stand for. Mahesh drives her again, and she advises him to tell his wife to stop giving baby Lasya honey as the bacterial spores are dangerous for infants.

At the orphanage, Tricia treats dozens of infants and toddlers who live in the multi-story building. It's a clean and spacious structure, but incredibly loud, with very little furniture and stone floors, so sound echoes and carries up the large central stairwell like a megaphone. The combination of fatigue and noise gives Tricia a headache, but she finds the children—each and every one—adorable and seemingly well looked after by their caregivers.

She treats several cases of scabies and dermatitis, and a two-year-old boy named Ajit with Harlequin ichthyosis, a rare condition where his body is covered with plates of hard, thick skin that cracks and splits apart. It pulls and distorts his facial features, affecting the shape of his ears, eyelids, nose, and mouth. Tricia has only seen one other case in her career, and takes her time examining him, as children with this condition can be prone to infections.

Being around all the infants and toddlers, playing with Ahmed, and talking to Mahesh about Lasya makes her nostalgic for the days when her own girls were little. They'd been her miracle babies. She'd first had to convince Jay to finally agree to kids, then spent years trying to get pregnant. Dr. Glowackie—terrible name, great doc—had worked his magic and finally, at age thirty-eight, she'd gotten pregnant with fraternal twins. A "geriatric pregnancy" it was offensively labeled. Regardless, she was elated to at last have a family.

She cradles fussy Ajit after the exam, and rocks him in a wooden rocking chair. She tries to hum a lullaby even though she can't sing for shit, but he eventually calms down and falls asleep. Tricia's eyes also begin to droop, and she nods off with him still cuddled in her lap.

Forty-five minutes later, the orphanage director gently shakes Tricia's shoulder to take Ajit, and tells Tricia to eat lunch. It's the longest sleep she's had since arriving in India.

At the end of a long day, she eats dinner alone in the hotel's Terrace Bar, where she indulges in three cocktails and the Asian Tapas menu. The evening view is pretty, with soft lighting and lush greenery, but the impenetrable wall of the city noise never ceases.

III.

Her body becomes so overly fatigued she has a constant headache and upset stomach. She settles into bed feeling like, yes, finally, the prescription pill, the exercise, it's going to happen. She'll at last fall into blissful unconsciousness. But after dozing for barely an hour, she begins to toss and turn. Her eyelids snap open like a plastic doll. She stares at the ceiling and tears fill her eyes, sliding down her temples into her hair.

She rises. Does more yoga, meditation, and dry-swallows another prescription pill, which only gives her restless leg syndrome—an irritating condition that feels like a deep, itchy ache, like her bones want to stretch themselves. Back in bed, she kicks, pulls, and twitches every few seconds until she wants to jump off her hotel balcony.

She rises again and takes two melatonin.

Her phone screen lights up with a new text from a group chat for her neighborhood friends.

Kristy: Don't forget wine night at my house tonight!

Kristy, the new queen bee of the neighborhood since Meredith moved.

Tricia watches the replies and banter about who is bringing what.

Kristy: Awesome! Everyone's confirmed! See you all at 7!

No one in the chat seems to remember Tricia is in India, or even notice that she hasn't responded.

She tells herself not to care, but can't stop reading the messages. The women aren't really her friends. She's social with them simply because of neighborhood proximity, as adults often do, but the neighborhood had changed a lot in the last few years. Couples splitting up and moving on, like Jessie and Dave and Meredith and Mike, and new people moving in. As for the rest of the women in the original circle, they'd always been fringe friendships by association, and lately, socializing with them felt like a performative chore on both sides.

Or maybe she was being phased out. Tricia couldn't decide whether this bothered her or not.

She'd never really had much in common with any of them beyond being neighbors. She and her kids were so much older than all of them and their kids, and she didn't give a shit about fashion, or decorating, or cooking, or social media, or even wine nights. All of which seemed very important to them.

She'd tried to fit in, but knew she didn't, and had always suspected the others were just being polite to include her. Her suspicion was confirmed recently when she'd overhead two women make a snarky comment about her shoes during wine night. Her beloved brown Birkenstock clogs that she wore year-round because they were so comfortable and matched everything.

Tricia had stepped around the corner of a room to grab her purse when two women in the kitchen started talking about her shoes. One woman had called all Birkenstocks *hideous*, and the second had laughed, *Ew! Right?* Kristy had shushed them, and when Tricia re-entered the room wearing her Birkenstocks, everyone carried on like nothing had happened.

Why is she thinking about this again? It was a petty, insignificant moment that shouldn't have any real estate in her mind.

And yet it does.

She turns out the lights once more and lays down.

She doesn't sleep.

THE NEXT MORNING, SHE NODS OFF during the car ride with Mahesh as he chatters about how close Lasya is getting to crawling.

Mahesh asks if she's okay.

I can't sleep, she answers. The time change is killing me.

At the clinic, she nods off between patients, and again while eating her egg and cheese during lunch.

Raj asks if she's okay.

I can't sleep, she answers. The time change is killing me.

IV.

Tricia hasn't slept for four nights. She doubles the prescription pills again, adds more melatonin tablets, and after tossing and turning for two hours, gets up and opens the minibar in her room. She selects a tiny bottle of whiskey and chugs it, setting her throat and belly on fire. She chugs a second one, rum this time. She hates rum and gags, fights not to throw it all back up onto the carpet.

She's a doctor and knows better than to take so much medication and add alcohol on top of it, but she can no longer think straight. She's growing desperate for any amount of sleep. Her body is physically shutting down. Her hands tremble during the day. She's unsteady on her feet, bumps into things, loses words while speaking.

Raj told her not to come to the clinic tomorrow, to stay in her hotel room to try and sleep. He's worried about her.

But she's going to the clinic anyway. If she sleeps during the day, it'll only be worse at night. She still has three more days to get through. She came here to be of use, and she won't be useful if she's sleeping all day.

The alcohol quickly mixes with the pills: the room begins to undulate and pulse around her. She tips and reaches for the edge of the desk but knocks the lamp and her workbag to the floor.

She sets the lamp back up, and kneels to collect the spilled items from her bag. Pen lights, half-used bottles of hand sanitizers, face masks, smashed tampons, and the book.

She puts everything back in the bag, except the book. *Stellaluna.*

She sits on the floor and flips through the pages and pictures she knows by heart without even looking at them. She never once actually read the book to either of her girls when they were little.

She closes the cover. She can't look at it right now. Returns it to her bag.

Are there bats in India? She doesn't know. Googles it, reads.

Indeed, bats are all over India, even in the cities. Little-nosed fruit bats are the most common.

She closes the browser and calls Jay, but he doesn't answer. He's probably still in surgery. She leaves him a voicemail.

Hey, honey, just calling to check in. Have a mean case of insomnia. Call me at seven your time, okay?

It's four in the afternoon at home; she texts both of the girls.

Tricia: What are you doing?

Lydia: making cookies with aunt kara

Claudia: watching funny tik toks

Her vision and brain become slippery, her eyelids heavy. Maybe? Finally?

She lowers herself to the floor, daring not to do more and disrupt the sleepiness pulling her body down like gravity.

She closes her eyes. Drifts. Floats.

She lightly dozes for only ten minutes, then wakes.

BACK AT *HELPING HANDS*, Tricia treats the first case of leprosy—actual *leprosy*—in her career for an elderly woman who already lost two fingers at the knuckle joints from the disease.

As she examines the woman, Tricia has a moment where she wonders if she's hallucinating. She calls Raj into the exam room for a quick consultation.

We get a few of these cases a month, he says.

She's relieved it isn't a hallucination, but doesn't tell Raj this.

V.

Tricia hasn't slept for five nights. When she rises to take another prescription pill in the bathroom, she accidentally drops it down the sink drain. It was her last one.

She leans over and peers down the dark, slimy tunnel, and spots the little white capsule resting on the edge of the plug latch. She jams her long index and middle fingers into the drain, carefully pinches the pill between her fingertips, and extracts it.

One side has a bit of gunk stuck to it, but Tricia doesn't care. She wipes it with a tissue, and swallows it down with another mini bottle of whiskey, re-stocked by housekeeping earlier that day. The booze charges alone on her bill will cost her a fortune.

She woozily thinks that if she had a wooden mallet, she would whack herself in the forehead with it until she fell unconscious, like a cartoon, just to get some sleep. The thought makes her laugh.

She leaves the bathroom and slumps onto the couch, switches on the television. She flips through endless channels with ads for skin lightening creams, finding nothing of interest.

She never watches TV before bedtime and has never allowed television sets in their bedrooms at home. The flickering glow of the screen makes her dizzy.

The room is stifling. She listlessly scrolls social media on her phone, watches a few stupid videos, and checks her text messages. Another question from Claudia asking where the band aids are. A funny meme from Jay about a dog, and a promise to call her at seven. And the damn neighborhood group chat.

Why is she still in it? Those women don't even like her, and really, she doesn't like them either.

Fuck it.

She sits up and types a quick message to Kristy:

Hey please permanently remove me and my hideous Birks from this group chat.

She taps "send," and laughs. Then deletes the chat and blocks all their numbers.

Strangely energized, she gets up and redresses in the clothes she wore earlier—a flowy broom skirt and light button up top that now smells like sweat and antiseptic. And her beloved Birkenstocks, fuck you very much.

She takes the elevator down to the lobby and exits the hotel and security gates unnoticed.

Outside, the air is thick and warm, and a light breeze ripples the skirt hem around her ankles. She follows the sidewalk east along Samrat Ashok Road as cars, motorcycles, busses, and green and yellow tuk-tuks whiz past her, rustling her frizzy hair. It's dangerous what she's doing, walking alone at night, but her prolonged fatigue is hindering her ability to care about anything, even her own safety.

She wonders what would happen if she died here. Who would tell Jay and the girls? Raj? Who would tell them when the orthodontist appointments are, where the band aids are kept?

Maybe that's the only hole she would leave in her family, like an office administrator.

The thought makes her terribly sad.

She keeps walking.

Across the street, Tricia sees a small pack of social dogs. They pay her no attention, and trot into some underbrush. She passes a mall and office building, and on Nagar Road, comes upon an ornately arched stone and metal gate entrance.

She stops and approaches. Beyond the locked gate is an expansive garden of shrubs and trees she can barely make out in the darkness. Just above her in a banyan tree, something squeaks, an insect-like pinging sound. She squints, and there, on one of the low branches, hangs a little fruit bat, just like the picture book.

Oh, my god, Tricia says, and smiles. Hello, Stellaluna.

The bat squeaks.

She grips the gate, staring at the real-life version of the pictures.

Are you here for me? she asks. We've been together a long time, haven't we?

More squeaks.

I don't know what you said, she replies. What do you want?

The squeaks turn to excited yapping.

Are you trying to tell me something important?

A man walks by and glances at her as she clings to the fence, talking to a bat like a lunatic.

Tricia ignores him, continues talking. I'm so tired, Stellaluna, she says. I can't sleep. I can't stop thinking about everything. Even you.

The bat flutters her wings, emits a single squeak.

I know, I know. Tricia shakes her head. I need to let you go.

The little bat suddenly drops from the branch and flaps her wings, swoops over Tricia's head, and disappears into the night.

Tricia cranes her neck, watching with a mixture of sadness and awe.

Goodbye, she whispers. Tears fill her eyes.

The sun is starting to rise.

She walks back to the Hyatt and takes the elevator to her room, where she showers and dresses for her last day.

VI.

Tricia returns to the clinic for her final morning shift. Raj pulls her aside and asks if she's fallen ill, or eaten something disagreeable.

She assures him there's no illness. She's just tired. That damn time difference. She tries to laugh it off.

Raj eyes her for a long moment, then unlocks a medicine cabinet. He selects an amber bottle, shakes out a pill, and presses it into her palm.

Please, he says, take this tonight. It's stronger than what you have in the states. It'll make you sleep, I promise. Geetha takes them sometimes.

Tricia smiles and thanks him.

When he leaves the room, she drops the pill back into the bottle. She doesn't need it. She knows what she needs to do now to help her sleep.

During lunch, Tricia goes back to B.S.S.K. to see Ajit.

But when she examines him, he's lethargic and has a low-grade fever. She hears faint crackles in both of his lungs. He's developed a respiratory infection in the few days since her first visit. He needs hospitalization.

She wraps his cracked, limp little body in a blanket and texts Mahesh to please return to the orphanage to get her. He arrives within a few minutes, and Tricia settles into the back seat holding Ajit on her lap, his head resting against her chest as he sucks his thumb. It feels wrong to ride in a car with an unrestrained child in her arms, but that's how it is here.

At Jehangir Hospital, in the center of the city, the emergency department admits Ajit to the Sunshine Pediatric Ward. Tricia goes with him. She texts Raj that she may be late for their goodbye dinner tonight at her hotel.

Ajit is given a PICC line for fluids and antibiotics, and he falls sleeps.

After consulting with a pediatric specialist, Tricia moves a chair next to Ajit's bed and strokes his dark, silky hair. After a few minutes, she removes the book about the little fruit bat from her bag.

She opens the cover and runs her fingers over the stamped check out slip.

Rochester Public Library
Due May 27, 2012

The girls were ten months old when it happened.

It was a Saturday afternoon. They were still living in their cramped, two-story brick house on the east side of the city. Their nanny didn't work weekends, and Jay had been called into the hospital for an emergency surgery, so Tricia was by herself.

Back then, she'd barely slept but a few hours each night, constantly up and down with Claudia, who was a terrible sleeper until her fourth birthday. That morning, she fed and dressed the twins in different colors of the same outfit, and strapped them into their car seats. She drove to the Rochester Public Library, not far from the Mayo Clinic where Jay worked, for baby story time.

They were late, of course, because Claudia started fussing minutes after Tricia pulled out of the garage, and cried all the way to the library. By the time Tricia got her calmed down and lugged both seats into the building, along with an oversized diaper bag, story time had already started.

She found a sliver of floor to sit on and wrangled both babies onto her lap, where they watched the librarian read from a brightly illustrated picture book about farm animals.

But within minutes, both girls started to cry, one after the other, like a perpetual canon in a song. She dug through her diaper for pacifiers but located neither. She'd forgotten them in the god damn console of her car.

Sweaty and flustered, Tricia returned the girls to their seats, and lugged them back outside. As she unlocked the doors, there, in the cup holder, were the two bright pink and yellow pacifiers where she'd left them. She clicked the seats onto their bases, popped one pacifier into each yowling mouth, slid into the driver's seat, and rested her head against the steering wheel.

She was so tired her joints ached.

The babies sucked away and slowly settled down.

God, she silently prayed, please have mercy on me, and make them fall asleep.

Just as she inserted the key to start her car, Tricia realized she'd forgotten to pick up a book she'd placed on hold. *Stellaluna.* A picture book about a little fruit bat their nanny recommended because she'd gotten it from the library once before and said the girls had really enjoyed it when she read it to them. But when Tricia tried to check it out again a few weeks ago, it wasn't available, so the librarian put it on hold for her. Part of the reason she'd brought the girls to story time that Saturday was to also pick up the book. Two birds, one stone. She was always trying to be as efficient and organized as possible.

She craned her neck to check the girls, and indeed, just as she'd prayed minutes before, they'd both drifted off to sleep.

Tricia turned around, stared at the library building, and sighed. If she moved their seats—yet again—they would wake up. Then their nap schedules would be completely disrupted, and the rest of the day would be, in a word, fucked.

Plus, she was just so damn tired. Her arms and shoulders ached from toting the heavy seats and bulky diaper bag around. The library would be closed the next day, and it was too far out of her way to get the book after work on Monday, before the hold expired. And she would never ask Jay to do it.

At the thought of him, Tricia shifted her gaze to the nearby Mayo hospital where he'd been called in to anesthetize an emergency appendectomy. Tricia never dealt with emergency cases as a dermatologist. Mostly cases of teenage acne and eczema. Sometimes melanoma, which was serious, but never emergent. Jay's work was forever an unspoken priority.

Even though he'd never explicitly said it, or actually did anything to make her feel that way, it was something she'd internalized on her own, regardless. She took care of the grocery shopping, dry-cleaning, pediatric appointments, library books, and everything else, often while dragging the babies along with her. Even though Jay had never asked or told her to.

She'd tried for so long to get pregnant. She had nothing to bitch about.

Tricia stared hard at the library once more, thinking about that damn book, waiting inside, with her name on a note stuck to the cover. The nanny would ask about it first thing Monday morning, Tricia just knew it.

She tightened her hands around the wheel, squeezing harder.

It was such a stupid thing to be angry about. It was just a book. Who cared whether or not she got it?

The vinyl twisted between her hands.

She did. She cared. She cared about stupid, pointless things like schedules and story time and that the nanny had been the one to discover a book about a little fruit bat her daughters had so enjoyed. Not her.

Tricia turned in her seat once more to glance at her still-sleeping babies and made a split-second decision. It would take less than a minute.

She quietly got out of the car, locked it, hurried across the parking lot, and went back into the library to the circulation desk. She gave the librarian her name, and while she waited, she realized how badly she needed to use the bathroom. The librarian returned with the book, stamped the due date on the checkout slip, and handed it to her. Less than sixty seconds.

As Tricia walked back toward the doors, she thought about how easy it would be to just step into the bathroom to use the toilet. She'd already come back inside, was ready to piss herself, and the women's restroom was literally ten steps from the doors.

She darted into the bathroom and the first empty stall, balanced the book on top of the chrome toilet roll dispenser, and ripped her pants down so fast she nearly tore the elastic band of her underwear. A powerful stream of urine shot into the stool water with a loud splatter, and she closed her eyes with sweet, merciful relief. She covered her face with her hands, and leaned her head against the stall wall, so tired, but so relieved, as urine continued to trickle.

She next remembers her forehead painfully smacking the toilet roll dispenser, and her eyes snapping open. She startled and flailed, momentarily disoriented in the narrow stall.

Holy shit, she'd dozed off. For how long? She wasn't sure. She quickly wiped herself, tucked the little book beneath her arm, washed her hands without even bothering to dry them, dashed back out of the bathroom, through the sliding doors, and into the parking lot to her car.

Only, a police vehicle with lights flashing was parked in front of it, and a uniformed officer and a woman stood next to one of the passenger doors.

The rest of the memory Tricia rarely, if ever, revisits, because it's too painful. Too shameful. Now, so many years later, she can only see fragments of the rest:

Unlocking the driver's side door. The girls still peacefully sleeping in their seats. Sitting in the back of the squad car. The face of the officer asking her questions and writing down her answers on a little flip pad. The written warning he'd given her after her tearful explanation of what happened.

After the officer let her go, she'd gotten into her car, stuck the picture book into her work bag laying on the front seat, shakily driven home, and shredded the warning.

She never told Jay about what had happened, never gave the book to the nanny, and never went back to the Rochester Public Library. Not even to return the book through the night deposit slot.

She'd kept the book in her bag for thirteen years, the little fruit bat like a reminder, a punishment, of the time she was so careless, and made such an unforgivable decision and mistake.

Back in Jehangir Hospital, in the Sunshine Pediatric Ward halfway around the world, her grinding fatigue lifts, and her mind feels sharper than it has in days.

Ajit awakens and looks at her. Blinks his beautiful, deep brown eyes.

Tricia turns to the first page of the book and begins to read aloud.

She had silently read the words to herself a thousand times, but never aloud, and they feel foreign in her mouth.

Tears roll down her cheeks, but she keeps going. When she finishes, she closes the book.

Ajit is still looking at her between the skin of his painfully cracked, misshapen eyelids. He reaches out and touches her wet cheek with a rough fingertip. She smiles and holds his hand. Then tucks the book beneath his arm, just like the little fruit bat in the Banyon tree told her to do.

The pediatric specialist returns, and he and Tricia discuss Ajit's case for a few more minutes.

Visiting hours end, and it's time for Tricia to leave.

She kisses Ajit's forehead goodbye, and he falls asleep once more, the book still under his arm.

TRICIA IS LATE FOR DINNER with Raj but they're able to eat a quick meal and say goodbye. He thanks her for all her work that week, especially with Ajit.

Did you have a good experience, he asks.

Yes, she says, it was a good experience.

VII.

Tricia boards her evening flight destined for a connection in Paris.

She buckles into her seat, closes her eyes, and falls into a deep, peaceful sleep.

Acknowledgments

Thank you to Cornerstone Press, the University of Wisconsin-Stevens Point, and Dr. Ross Tangedal for believing in this collection, and to the editorial team of Ellie Atkinson, McKenna Bartel, Gwen Goetter, and the rest of the editorial team. A special thank you to Ari Pinder for the gorgeous cover art, and to Sam Bjork and Sophie McPherson in media/sales.

Thank you to the editors and publishers of the following literary journals where several of these stories first appeared in different form: *The Coachella Review*, *The Chaffey Review*, *Midwestern Gothic*, *The Milo Review*, and *Northwind Literary*.

Thank you to the talented fellow writers who read early drafts of many of these stories over the years and provided valuable feedback, but especially to Mathieu Cailler, Donald Quist, and Jackie Jensen.

Thank you to my beloved family and friends for always supporting me, and letting me borrow story ideas from your endlessly interesting lives.

And thank you, dear reader, always.

Kali White VanBaale is the author of three novels, including *The Monsters We Make*, an All Iowa Reads finalist, as well as short stories, essays, and articles. She's the recipient of an American Book Award, an Eric Hoffer Book Award, two State of Iowa major artist grants, and an Iowa Author Award. She's the editor-at-large of the *Past Ten* essay journal and *The Past Ten* print anthology. She's a core faculty member of the Lindenwood University MFA in Writing Program where she was named adjunct professor of the year. She lives in Iowa with her family. www.kaliwhite.com